Torey glared at him. "I'm sure it had nothing to do with your infernal teasing when we were kids, *or* your disgusting remarks when we were in high school."

"And then there was that kiss." Bart grinned. "That really set your hair on end, didn't it? One little kiss. From the ruckus you raised, it was more like I had..." He laughed softly, letting the idea dangle and saturate Torey's senses. "Know what I'd like to do right now?"

"I have an idea, yes."

"Now, wherever would you have learned ideas like that? No one gossips about Torey Lancaster, do they?"

"They have no reason to."

"Exactly. I have a feeling *that* part of your education has been sorely neglected, honey. I'd sure volunteer for the job anytime you said the word."

"Don't hold your breath."

"Let's go upstairs," he whispered. "I'd love to find out what's under these pretty clothes, and you could do a little exploring of your own. We could while away a rainy afternoon...."

Dear Reader,

Welcome to Silhouette Desire! Naturally, I think you've made a spectacular choice because, for me, each and every Silhouette Desire novel is a delightful, romantic, unique book. And once you start reading your selection I *know* you'll agree!

Silhouette Desire is thrilling romance. Here you'll encounter the joys and even some of the tribulations of falling in love. You'll meet characters you'll get to know and like . . . and heroes you'll get to know and *love*. Sensuous, moving, compelling, these are all words you can use to describe Silhouette Desire. But remember, words are not enough—you must *read* and get the total experience!

And there is something wonderful in store for you this month: *Outlaw*, the first in Elizabeth Lowell's WESTERN LOVERS series. It tells the story of rough-and-tough Tennessee Blackthorne . . . a man of fiery passions and deep emotions.

Of course, *all* of February's Silhouette Desire books are terrific—don't miss a single one! Until next month . . .

All the best,

Lucia Macro
Senior Editor

JACKIE
MERRITT

MAVERICK HEART

SILHOUETTE *Desire*®

Published by Silhouette Books New York

America's Publisher of Contemporary Romance

SILHOUETTE BOOKS
300 East 42nd St., New York, N.Y. 10017

MAVERICK HEART

ISBN: 0-373-05622-2

First Silhouette Books printing February 1991

Printed in the U.S.A.

Books by Jackie Merritt

Silhouette Desire

Big Sky Country #466
Heartbreak Hotel #551
Babe in the Woods #566
Maggie's Man #587
Ramblin' Man #605
Maverick Heart #622

JACKIE MERRITT

and her husband live just outside of Las Vegas, Nevada. An accountant for many years, Jackie has happily traded numbers for words. Next to family, books are her greatest joy, both for reading and writing.

One

Torey Lancaster slammed the door and tore through the house to the study. Her boots were caked with mud and her hat was dripping rain. Ordinarily she would never have brought so much of the spring storm inside with her, but she was furious and not thinking about anything but stopping Bart Scanlon.

Cursing under her breath, Torey located the sheriff's telephone number and dialed it. "Lacey? Let me speak to Roscoe, please. This is Torey Lancaster."

A few seconds later Torey had Sheriff Roscoe Ledbetter on the line. "Roscoe, I want something done about Scanlon Logging Company. Bart's building a road right next to my fence line!"

"On his own land?"

"I don't care whose land it is! Bart's a rapist, and I want him stopped!"

"He's a *what?*"

Torey groaned. "I only meant that he's raping the land. Roscoe, I don't want a damned logging road ten feet from my fence line. There must be a way to stop this . . . this disfigurement."

"This what?"

"Oh, Lord! Roscoe, you're the law around here. Will you do something about this or not?"

"Torey, what can I do? The man's on his own land. He can dig up the entire mountain and his part of the valley if he wants to."

"I don't care if he digs up the damned mountain! I just don't want him running a logging road right next to my fence!" Torey took an impatient, exasperated breath. "Oh, forget it, Roscoe. I'll go and see Bart myself."

Torey put the phone down, then noticed the water dripping from her hat brim. She got up and yanked the old gray hat off, which released the wealth of hair that had been tucked up under it. The mud on her cowboy boots caught her eye, and she quickly sat back down and pulled them off, too.

Damn Bart Scanlon, anyway. He always had been an overbearing jerk, from the time he'd been the nasty little boy on the next ranch, through high school, and each and every time she had the misfortune of running into him at the present. Bart didn't smile, he patronized. He never just said a friendly hello, his startling blue eyes undressed a woman!

Carrying her boots and hat, Torey stalked from the study and down the hall to her bedroom. The beauty of the environment might not mean anything to Bart Scanlon, but it did to her. In her opinion, he was destroying his land by logging it, but that was his business. That wretched machine tearing an ugly gash in the pasture ten feet from her fence line was hers! It was in full view of her house, too, a blot on a scenic sweep of the countryside that she had always found pacifying, comforting.

After a quick shower Torey dressed in gray slacks and a matching sweater. She ran a careless brush through her shoulder-length auburn curls, dabbed on a little makeup, blinked her large gray eyes at her reflection in the mirror and decided she'd do. She wasn't driving over to the Scanlon place to impress its owner; she was going to discuss a very important issue.

On her way outside, Torey veered to the kitchen. A middle-aged woman was cutting up vegetables for the beef stew she was preparing for dinner. "I'm going out for a while, Lorna. I shouldn't be long."

Torey had inherited Lorna Myers right along with the ranch when her grandparents had died within a year of one another a few years back. Lorna had worked on the ranch for a long time, and was as close to family as Torey had now. She was friend, confidante and a marvelous cook, and having someone else in the big rambling ranch house was important to Torey.

"All right, Torey. It's still raining out. Do you need a jacket?"

"I don't think so. It's not cold out, and this sweater will be plenty. See you later."

The hard rain of an hour ago had subsided to a fine drizzle. Torey decided on the pickup rather than the car and climbed up behind the wheel. She started the motor and switched on the windshield wipers, then turned the vehicle around and drove away.

To reach the Scanlon house, it was necessary to leave Lancaster land, drive about a mile on the highway, then traverse a long driveway on Scanlon property. Torey knew there was no guarantee that Bart would be at the house, but it had been raining since early morning. While the sloppy weather hadn't prevented that disgustingly enormous tractor from working on that new road, Torey suspected it might have shut down Bart's logging operation. She hoped so. She was in the right frame of mind to deal with this right now, and she didn't want to have to delay the unavoidable confrontation with Bart.

She pulled up beside the house and turned off the ignition key. Three large dogs of doubtful parentage rushed the pickup, barking and throwing themselves around as if a known cattle rustler had driven up. "Oh, shut up," Torey yelled irately through the window, but she wasn't brave enough to get out. Irked, she leaned on the horn until she saw the front door of the house opening.

It was the master of the house, himself, Bart Scanlon. She rolled down the window and said coldly, "Would you please call off your dogs?"

"Torey Lancaster. Well, well, well."

There it was again, that condescending smile. Bart was lucky he was good-looking, because he had the personality of a slug. Without looks, he'd be nothing, a big zero. As it was, she'd heard plenty of stories about Bart and the local belles, Lord save *her* from such a fate! She'd despised Bart as a boy and she still couldn't stand his arrogance.

Her haughty glance took in his dark, unruly hair and lean, lithe body in faded denim shirt and jeans. "I'd like to talk to you about something, if you'd be good enough to pen up these animals."

Bart bent over and patted the nearest dog. "They wouldn't hurt a flea," he drawled.

"No doubt. But they all look like they'd adore having me for dinner."

Straightening up, Bart gave her a lazy once-over. "Well, you do look rather tasty, now that you mention it. I might try a bite, myself, one of these days."

Despite a rigid determination to not let Bart get to her, Torey felt too much warmth in her cheeks. "Fat chance," she snapped.

Grinning maddeningly, Bart gave a low command to the dogs. The trio immediately became silent sentinels. "Get out and come in the house if you want to talk. In case you haven't noticed, it's raining."

He was getting wet, which tickled Torey. But the subject she'd come to discuss—or debate—was important enough to forego the pleasure of watching rain trickle down into Bart Scanlon's shirt collar. Torey reached for the door handle with one eye on the dogs.

"They're harmless," Bart assured her, opening her door before she could.

Torey stepped to the ground. "They sure don't look it," she retorted dryly. Bart led the way to the house and held the door for Torey to precede him in. Compared to her house, which was always in order because of Lorna's good care, the Scanlon house was a disaster. The foyer contained a row of wall pegs that were overloaded with jackets and hats, and, Torey saw, some kind of leather harness and a coil of rope. There was mud on the floor, which could have been tracked in that day. But there was enough of it that Torey suspected no one had applied a broom or vacuum cleaner for weeks.

Bart brought her to the living room. Two pairs of shoes littered carpeting that had definitely seen better days, a lone woolen stocking draped a chair arm, newspapers and magazines were scattered all over the place, and soft drink cans and a bowl of popcorn sat on the coffee table. Bart didn't live alone. He had two younger brothers, eighteen-year-old twins, Rich and Rob, to contend with, and it was obvious that none of the Scanlons worried too much about a clean house.

Bart didn't even appear to notice the condition of the room. "Have a seat," he invited, and grabbing a handful of popcorn, plopped down on the couch. "Want some?"

"No, thank you." Eyeing her choices, Torey settled for the chair with the stocking adornment. As soon as she sat down, a large yellow cat jumped onto her lap. Startled at first, she then let the purring cat curl up on her thighs.

Bart was watching with a bemused expression. "Corky's a real friendly cat."

"So I see."

Bart popped another fluffy kernel into his mouth. "Of course, he always looks for the softest thing in the room to sleep on. If there was a goose-down pillow in here, your thighs wouldn't stand a chance."

Torey nearly choked. Even as a boy Bart had known just what to say to make her crazy. On the schoolbus he'd pulled her hair, called her Tortilla Torey and swiped her books and lunchpail, tormenting her to tears. In high school the nickname had changed to Torrid Torey, and the torment had been in the form of wolf whistles and lewd remarks. One time he'd had the audacity to kiss her, and then when she'd tried to sock him in the jaw, he'd caught her hands and held them, laughing while she screamed and called him names.

Now, it took every ounce of control she could summon to stop herself from laying the few she'd overlooked that day on him. Unceremoniously Torey dumped the cat on the floor, which raised a squawk of protest from Corky and a laugh from Bart. "I didn't come over here to amuse you," she said waspishly.

"Probably not. But you do it so well, honey."

"And you..." Torey bit her tongue. If she started on him the way she would like to, they never would get to the road. She cleared her throat. "You have a tractor working on a new road...."

"A bulldozer, Torey."

"Whatever it is, it's making a horrible mess."

Bart nodded agreeably. "Probably looks that way."

"I talked to the operator. He said you were building the road for your logging trucks."

"And that's the truth," Bart said with mock solemnity. He sat back, his eyes on Torey. "Apparently something about that is bothering you. I don't think you've been over here for...what, Torey? Six, seven years?"

"I haven't kept track." Torey acknowledged a spurt of nervousness. She was, after all, on Scanlon land and about to complain about something Bart had every legal right to do. But why should she have to put up with an eyesore of a road and roaring diesel trucks raising dust all summer? "May I ask why you chose that particular spot for the road?"

Bart nodded with sudden understanding. "Ah, I see the problem. You don't like the road being so close to Lancaster land."

"It's going to be a blight on the landscape," Torey said sharply. "You've only just started the road. Before it's too late, would you possibly consider putting it somewhere else?"

"Can you see it from your house?"

"Of course I can see it from my house! It will ruin the best view I've got in any direction."

Bart got up, a lazy uncoiling of lithe muscles that Torey found herself staring at. The man had a perfect body, long and lean and blatantly apparent in the snug softness of old denim. There was a small ragged hole just below the left pocket of his jeans, which allowed just a tiny peek at the sinewy thigh beneath it. A worn leather belt connected at the top of his fly with a showy brass buckle. His shirt was open three buttons down from the collar, and a tuft of black hair protruded from the gap.

Torey drew a strangely alarmed breath and brought her gaze up to his face, only to see a smug look of comprehension. Her cheeks burned to a deep crimson. It was one of the most embarrassing moments of her life. To be caught staring at Bart Scanlon's body was a humiliation beyond imagination. She couldn't believe it when he didn't rub her nose in it with some scathing remark.

"It's all about cost, Torey. I laid out various routes and made cost studies all winter for that road."

With a struggle, she regained a little aplomb. "Money isn't everything. What about the environmental impact?"

"Roads are rarely pretty things."

"Yes, but why should I have to endure an eyesore to save you a few dollars?"

Bart smirked. "A few dollars? Do you have any idea of the outlay for a new road? That dozer and operator out there are running two hundred dollars an hour. Once the initial roadway is punched out, there'll be grading to do, then gravel to haul in. We're not talking about a few bucks, Torey. I chose the most level, least obstructed strip of the ranch because it will save me *thousands* of dollars."

"Wonderful," she muttered caustically, seeing defeat on the horizon. "I don't know why you're logging your land, anyway. You're depleting its value. This ranch must certainly make as much profit as mine."

Bart smiled smoothly. "But you don't have two younger brothers who want to go to medical school."

"Oh." Torey's fighting spirit deflated a notch. "Rob and Rich want to be doctors," she said weakly.

"In the worst way, and I'm going to see that they succeed. They're starting college this fall. Four years of college, then medical school. Maybe they'll want to specialize, which would mean further education."

"Taking on that much expense is very noble of you," Torey mumbled. Not once had it ever occurred to her that

Bart Scanlon might have some redeeming qualities. He'd been a thorn in her side ever since she'd been seven years old, orphaned and brought to the ranch by her grandparents.

Well, it was obvious she was wasting her time. Bart wasn't going to change the route of the logging road, and maybe she couldn't blame him. It was difficult to reconcile her own preferences with Bart's familial philanthropy, however. The fact remained that she was going to have to live with a ravaged landscape, and envisioning the Scanlon twins as physicians was small personal comfort. Rob and Rich had the same kind of reputation Bart had had in high school, handsome but wild as March hares. The thought of them getting through college, let alone medical school, was almost ludicrous.

But apparently Bart didn't feel that way. With a long-suffering sigh, Torey got to her feet. "I'll be running along. Thanks for hearing me out."

"Anytime, honey. You perk up the old place."

That outlaw grin was on full throttle. And Bart Scanlon's eyes were so blue they looked electric. He needed a haircut, she decided, glad to find something not quite right about his flawless masculinity. His sassy compliment grated on her nerves. After their over twenty years of ill-concealed hostility, blarney about her looking good enough to eat and perking up the place didn't set quite right. "*You* could perk the old place up yourself with a little elbow grease," she drawled sarcastically.

He raised an eyebrow. "Applying for the job?"

"Hardly!"

Bart laughed, low and suggestively. "Never can find one of those old-fashioned women who wants to move in and mother me."

Torey tossed out a deprecating laugh. "If one were to listen to gossip, Scanlon, you hardly spend much time with the motherly type." She started for the door.

"But, of course, *you* would never listen to gossip."

A hand came around her and held the door closed. Torey's spine tingled and her pulse picked up speed. "What are you doing?"

"Inhaling. You sure smell good, honey."

Torey didn't know whether to turn around and sock him or bluff her way out of this with her back to him. So far he hadn't touched her, but he was close enough to move in very quickly. "I'd like to leave," she said, putting a strong demand in her voice.

"Torrid Torey," he murmured softly, and she felt him inch a little closer. He infuriated Torey, but then Bart always had. She had learned long ago how crude he was, but that tingling in her spine was something brand new. "How come we never got along, honey?"

His nerve amazed her, and she turned around to glare at him. "I'm sure it had nothing to do with your infernal teasing when we were kids, *or* your disgusting remarks when we were in high school."

"And then there was that kiss." Bart grinned. "That really set your hair on end, didn't it? One little kiss. From the ruckus you raised it was more like I had..." He laughed softly, letting the idea dangle and saturate Torey's senses. Color flooded her face when she saw his gaze narrow on her mouth.

"Don't get any foolish ideas, Bart," she warned, and was shocked by the breathiness of her own voice.

The corners of his eyes crinkled in amusement. "What's foolish to you might not be to me." He brought his head down, and Torey turned hers quickly, avoiding the kiss she'd seen coming. The evasion didn't seem to deter him a whole lot; she felt his lips moving on her hair.

"Bart...don't," she whispered.

"Know what I'd like to do right now?"

"I have an idea, yes."

He chuckled softly and whispered in her ear, and his breath raised goose bumps on Torey's skin. "Now, wherever would you have learned ideas like that? No one gossips about Torey Lancaster, do they?"

"They have no reason to."

"Exactly. I have a feeling *that* part of your education has been sorely neglected, honey. I'd sure volunteer for the job anytime you said the word."

Torey stiffened. "Don't hold your breath. Bart, let me leave. This is ridiculous."

"Let's go upstairs," he whispered. "I'd love to find out what's under these pretty clothes, and you could do a little exploring of your own. We could while away a rainy afternoon...."

"Just stop it! I'm not going upstairs or anywhere else with you. It's no damned wonder I've tried to avoid you. You've got the finesse of a bull in a china shop!"

He laughed, a rich sound of genuine relish. He was getting such a kick out of this, Torey wanted to smack him. She never had enjoyed wrestling matches with men, and the strange, furtive thrills in her own body were adding to her discomfort.

Bart planted a big smooch on her cheek. "All right, sweetheart. The fun's over. You can leave." He stepped back.

"Well, thank you very much," she said peevishly. She knew Bart had followed her out the door and to the small front porch, but she didn't look back. Not until she saw the three dogs lying between her and her pickup. One emitted a low growl, and Torey stopped dead in her tracks, then threw an angry glare over her shoulder. "Would you do something about these beasts?"

"Blackie, Biscuit, Sweetpea!" he called.

"Sweetpea?"

Bart shrugged with boyish perplexity, as though he had no idea how that ugly hound had come by the name. Torey shook her head in amazement, then bounded for the safety of her pickup.

Two

On the short drive home Torey was beset by some extraordinary thoughts. What had those weird tingles and shivers been all about during Bart's pass? Oh, she knew what they were, but to experience sexual response to Bart Scanlon was downright astounding. Sure, he was good-looking, but he hadn't just turned good-looking overnight. He'd been a handsome little brat of a boy and a head-turner in high school. Ten years later, why should she all of a sudden feel crazy things for a man she still found as irritating as a burr under a saddle?

Twenty-eight wasn't old enough for the change of life to start affecting her hormone level, so Torey couldn't pin her aberration on anything so beyond her control. No, those tingles and shivers had been because of Bart, simply because he was one sexy guy, and if she'd noticed that before, she hadn't let herself admit it.

Electric-blue eyes, yet. Why had she gotten so poetic over eyes she'd seen hundreds of times and usually when they were full of mischief because she was cringing over some idiotic joke of Bart's? A joke or an insult. He'd teased her to tears more times than she cared to remember.

And yet, when he could have made some smart remark because he'd caught her staring, he'd let it pass. That was very uncharacteristic of Bart Scanlon. Oh, he'd gotten a few gibes in, that one about her soft thighs, for example. Bart never ever forgot that he was a man when talking to a woman, Torey realized. He never forgot that *she* was female, and he seemed to love reminding her of it. In fact, now that she really thought about it, the damned man made her feel more like a woman than anyone else she'd ever been around!

She frowned all the way home. This was a startling turn and Torey wasn't sure she liked it. She was currently dating Steve Johnson, a veterinarian who'd recently moved to Stanton, the nearest town. Steve was a nice guy, good-looking, too, but she'd never gotten all shivery around him. Not like she had today with Bart Scanlon.

The hardest part of the episode to assimilate was a desire to experience those unnerving shivers again. Now, why would a woman purposely hope for another bout of chills? Disgusted with herself, Torey screeched the pickup to a halt beside the house and slammed the door good and hard when she got out.

Lorna was in the living room, reading the newspaper, when Torey went in. The older woman folded the paper and set it aside. "You weren't gone very long."

"I went over to Scanlon's place." Torey sprawled in a chair, her legs stretched out in front of her, the frown still firmly in place.

"Because of that machine out there?"

"I hate where he's building that new road. But Bart said it's the most cost-efficient spot on his ranch to put it."

"Well, maybe it is. But what does he need it for?"

"To haul his damned logs off the mountain. Lorna, did you know that Rob and Rich Scanlon are going off to college this fall to begin a medical education? Bart said they both want to be doctors."

Lorna laughed. "Those two scamps?" Her brown eyes lit up. "I just remembered something. Bart wanted to be a doctor, too, you know."

"He did?"

"You don't remember when he quit college and came home after his dad died?"

"I sure don't. Where was I when that was going on?"

"Well, let me see. Bart's a few years older than you, but you must have been in college, too. Your first year, probably. Yes, I remember the story now. The twins were pretty young, about seven or eight, I'd guess. When their father died, the State tried to put the boys in a foster home. Bart said no way, and gave up his education to take care of them."

"No kidding?" Torey sighed then. "Well, it's little wonder I didn't pay any attention to it even if I heard about it. I despised Bart in those days."

Lorna smiled. "In those days? When did that change?"

"It hasn't!" Torey declared emphatically, and got to her feet. "I think I'll do a little bookwork before dinner."

Lorna picked up the paper again. "It will be ready in about an hour."

"Fine. Just give me a yell."

Torey went to the study and closed the door. She hated bookwork and needed all her powers of concentration to accomplish anything. After she sat at the desk for fifteen minutes and had done little else but fidget, she put her pen down. Those few minutes with Bart hovering over her had left a mark.

In the first place, there was more to Bart than she'd ever given him credit for. So, he'd wanted to be a doctor. That was something she hadn't known, or if anyone had ever mentioned it, Torey hadn't absorbed the information. At any rate, it was probably the underlying reason why he was so determined to give Rob and Rich a medical education.

Torey tried to visualize Bart Scanlon as an M.D., wearing a white coat and a stethoscope around his neck. The image wouldn't quite gel. Bart was pure country, fitting the blue jeans and scuffed cowboy boots he wore like a uniform. Had she ever seen him in anything else? Oh, sometimes the jeans were new and the boots shined, but no, in over twenty years, she had never seen Bart in anything but jeans and boots.

Of course, she'd tried very hard not to see Bart at all. It happened every so often, despite her strong personal preference to the contrary. In Stanton occasionally, at one local function or another, she and Bart would come face to face. He never failed to rile her, if by no more than one of those arrogant outlaw grins of his. If he got a chance to speak to her, he managed to give her a maddening dig of one kind or another, mostly, Torey now realized, relating to her gender.

The man was sick, she decided, obsessed with sex. Yes, that was it. All these years his gibes and innuendo had been sexually-oriented, and she should have realized that a long, long time ago.

And she wanted another case of Scanlon's brand of shivers? Was she sick, too?

Dispirited, Torey got up and went to the window. She could see the huge yellow tractor on the other side of her fence, silent and unmoving now. The operator must have quit for the day, she realized, studying the long, ugly, dark gash of overturned earth. Bart's determination to put his brothers through medical school was commendable, but he wasn't the only one who was going to pay for it. There were other methods of payment besides cold cash, and she, Torey Lancaster, and any future residents of Lancaster land were all going to bear the burden of the defiled view. If she was petty for resenting it, then so be it. She couldn't help her feelings, any more than Bart could help his.

She and Bart had always been at odds, and certainly nothing had changed in that regard. But something *had* changed. Why she should suddenly be seeing Bart Scanlon as a man was an irritating puzzle, but that's what had occurred. And the more Torey thought about it, the more dejected she became. She would never, ever get personally involved with Bart Scanlon.

Or, would she?

At that time of year Torey had only one man working on the ranch. During spring branding and fall roundups she put on extra help. But chores were easily handled the rest of the year by herself and one employee. The Lancaster ranch was of moderate size, fifteen hundred acres that encompassed a good portion of the valley and the south tip of the mountain that Bart was logging. On a clear day she could hear echoing sounds from the mountain, the low growls and rumbles of engines and once in a while, even a distant, unintelligible shout.

Torey watched the road's progress daily, not at all pleased that once it was completed, diesel trucks loaded with logs would be passing very close to her house. Her hands were tied on the matter, she knew, but that only increased her frustration.

Frustration of another nature was also keeping her on edge. Try as she might, she couldn't stop thinking about Bart. She'd gone out with Steve three different evenings since the incident, but it was Bart who had started haunting her dreams. She likened herself to the proverbial moth after an open flame, she tried reasoning with her libido, but at the oddest moments her knees would get weak from the memory of Bart inhaling her scent and the sensation of having his tall, lean body crowding hers.

Torey found herself watching for Bart's dusty black pickup on the road when she went to town, and keeping an eye on the new road site. She kept a safe distance, but she would stop whatever task she was involved with and watch him talking and gesturing to the tractor operator. Bart moved like a cat, she decided. Like a sleek jungle cat on the prowl.

After that one day of rain the weather had turned warm, and sometimes she spotted him in a shirt with the sleeves cut out. His arms were dark and heavily muscled, a laboring man's arms, and she began wondering how the rest of him looked under his clothes. Were his legs dark, too? He didn't have an ounce of flab anywhere that she could detect. His belly was tight and flat, and his hips were lean.

He usually wore a hat, a disreputable old thing that looked worse than the one she wore for work. But it shadowed his face and made his eyes a mystery. Then one day she was in the house when she saw his pickup stop beside the tractor, and without even thinking about what she was doing, Torey raced for the binoculars and ran to the privacy of her bedroom window. She adjusted the lens and caught Bart's face dead center.

His changing expressions, from sobriety to laughter, ripped through her. She saw the riveting blue of his eyes and the flash of white teeth as he talked and grinned. His mouth was so sexy it was sinful, and she tried hard to remember the long ago kiss she'd fought so hard against. Disappointingly it was only a ten-year-old blur of teenaged awkwardness in her mind.

Realizing she was breathing as though she'd run a foot race, Torey lowered the binoculars and sat on the edge of her bed. This was getting out of hand. Her palms were sweaty and her mouth was dry. What was happening to her?

The binoculars in her lap angered her. If she wanted something from Bart Scanlon, all she had to do was ask. He'd made enough hints and crude, suggestive remarks over the years that she knew he wouldn't retreat from a personal overture. In fact, hadn't he volunteered for the job of improving her "neglected" education?

The thought was appalling. Torey winced at a mental image of her attempting to sweet-talk Bart. He'd probably take anything she had the guts to offer, then destroy her with one of those patronizing smiles. No, that definitely was not the answer.

But what was? She'd tried everything to drive him from her mind. And look what she'd done, spied on him with a pair of binoculars!

Opening the bottom drawer of her nightstand, Torey shoved the binoculars under some books, then pushed the drawer closed. Rising, Torey prowled around her room. The problem was, Bart thought of her as the girl next door. He had to have as many memories of her as she had of him, but the two of them had always been so contradictory, those memories were hardly heartwarming. For either of them, no doubt. Their antagonistic childhood had set the tone for their teen years, and it had gone on from there.

Maybe what she'd better do was decide just what she did want from him. A one-woman admiration society was too adolescent. She either had to get Bart deeper into or completely out of her system. Rationally, she'd much rather get him out of it, but she didn't seem to have the power to do that.

If she knew him better...?

Yes, that might do it. Maybe all it would take would be another dose of his overbearing personality to rid herself of this nightmare. But how could she suddenly start seeking out someone she'd avoided for twenty years?

And, by all means, do it without being obvious. That was exceedingly crucial. She would not knowingly put herself in a position of looking like a fool, not even to squelch this ridiculous anxiety in her body. Well, maybe not anxiety. Ache? Unrest? Desire? Just what was it besides a pull she couldn't stop herself from responding to? It was like Bart was exuding some sort of arcane magnetism, and she was being tugged toward it against her will.

Laughing weakly, Torey nervously brushed her hair back from her face with both hands. It was a gesture of helplessness, which really alarmed her. She'd never considered herself a helpless individual. Except in her dealings with Bart, of course, and until recently, she'd ignored that particular weakness by avoiding him. It seemed almost insane to deliberately walk into a lion's den.

But it was also, she knew with disturbing clarity, impossible to do nothing. She had to find out what was drawing her to Bart Scanlon after all these years. "You *could* get burned," she whispered, afraid of Bart deep down. He was a high-voltage individual, and there was no question that she could end up a scorched cinder fooling around with Bart.

It was a chance she had to take, Torey decided. Thinking hard, she continued to pace. How could she run into Bart more often? He lived right on the next ranch, but she certainly had no idea of his routines or habits. It was sensible to assume that he spent most of his days at the logging site, and it wasn't too out of line to envision herself taking a horseback ride and sort of wandering along and stopping to take a look at the operation. Yes, she could do that. Once, at least.

For that matter, she could go outside right now and approach the fence. Bart would come over, if only to torment her. But she couldn't go to the fence without a reason. She couldn't stand around and make small talk; that was something she had never attempted with Bart, and he'd see through it in a second. He'd probably come right out and ask her what she really wanted, teasing her with that maddening grin, looking through her clothes with those piercing blue eyes.

Torey remembered his seductive invitation. *Let's go upstairs and while away the rainy afternoon. I'd like to see what's under those pretty clothes, and you could do a little exploring, too.*

She dampened her suddenly dry lips. That was exactly the crux of this whole thing: She wished she had climbed those stairs!

Torey pressed trembling fingertips to her throbbing temples. This was insane. Lusting after Bart Scanlon was unbelievably insane!

"Torey?"

Lorna had rapped, then opened the bedroom door. Torey gave herself a quick mental shake, relieved that Lorna couldn't know what outrageous thoughts she had interrupted. "Yes, Lorna?"

"Bart Scanlon is here. He wants to see you for a minute."

Torey stared numbly. While she'd been soul-searching and making some very disheartening discoveries, Bart must have hopped the fence. Why? He didn't just drop in, or he never had before. The last time she could remember him on Lancaster land was long before her grandfather died, and that was five years ago. Bart had attended the funeral, he and Rob and Rich, but the Scanlons hadn't come back to the house like dozens of other neighbors had.

"Should I tell him you're busy?" Lorna questioned.

"Oh...no, of course not. I'll go see what he wants." Giving herself a quick glance in the mirror, then wishing she hadn't because she certainly didn't look her best, Torey hurried past Lorna and on through the house.

"He's in the kitchen," Lorna called, indicating to Torey that Bart had knocked at the back door.

Before reaching the kitchen doorway, Torey slowed her fast pace and took a deep breath. Then, pasting a completely disinterested expression on her face, she walked into the room. "Hello, Bart."

He'd been leaning against the counter, and he straightened up from his relaxed slouch. His hat was in place on his head and there was dust and dirt on his clothes, making it obvious to Torey that he'd interrupted his workday for this call.

"Hi. I was just out looking at the road and had an idea."

"Oh?"

"I really never gave its proximity to your house any thought until you complained...."

"Oh, please! I didn't really complain. I merely..."

He grinned. "Like hell you didn't. Anyway, I thought maybe a row of poplars along your fence line might be better to look at than the road."

"Poplars? But they would block the entire view."

Bart shrugged. "You can't have everything. If the road's such an eyesore, poplars would conceal it pretty well. I'm willing to pay half the cost of putting them in."

Torey's eyebrow lifted. "Mature trees would cost quite a lot."

"I was thinking more along the line of *moderately* mature," Bart amended with an amused twinkle in his eyes.

"Oh, I see. Well, I'm not sure."

"Think about it. If you decide to go ahead with it, let me know." Touching the brim of his hat with his forefinger, Bart started for the door.

He was leaving, Torey realized, and she'd played her normal role of disdainful neighbor so well, she'd gained nothing except the start of a stomach ache. Uncharacteristically she followed him out the door, searching frantically for something to say, finally coming up with, "How much longer before the road is finished?"

Bart stopped. "About another three weeks." He grinned. "Why? Planning on a little sabotage?"

"Hardly!" she retorted sharply, then realizing that he was teasing her, she formed a smile. "That's something that never occurred to me, to be perfectly honest. Thanks for the idea."

Bart's laughter rang out. "You wouldn't even begin to know how to sabotage a road, honeybun."

She gave him an arch look. "I could learn, couldn't I? I'm a fast learner, Scanlon."

The smile faded from his lips and his blue eyes narrowed on her as he realized she was flirting. Torey Lancaster flirting with him? His pulse quickened appreciatively. "You might be, at that," he said softly. "But I can think of a more exciting subject to put your time to than the fine art of sabotage."

"And what would that be?" Torey knew she was really playing with fire with that question. Every cell in her body knew it, in fact.

Bart couldn't believe this. He'd always gotten a kick out of teasing Torey because she'd never failed to get spitting mad. Instead of ignoring him or laughing about it, she'd egged him on by getting mad. Underlying all the tomfoolery, he'd always had a yen for Miss Torey Lancaster. She was such a prissy little thing in so many ways, although there was nothing prissy about her looks. A man could get lost in her big, wet-slate eyes, and he'd always wanted to thread his fingers through her mass of auburn hair. As for her figure, well, he sure couldn't find anything wrong with

full, rounded breasts, a tiny waist and a great looking der-
riere.

His voice dropped to silky sensuality. "Maybe we should
discuss the possibilities over a drink tonight. I could pick
you up around seven."

"Seven." Torey was beginning to lose courage. A date
with Bart Scanlon could be the most dangerous outing
she'd ever dared. And yet, her adrenalin-charged body was
urging her to agree. Actually, her brain was telling her to
beat a hasty retreat, while her hormones were acting up
something awful. That erotic tingling was tormenting her
spine again, and this time, it was she doing the inhaling.
Bart smelled like sweat and grime, hardly the kind of odor
one would normally label arousing. But it was. His musky
maleness had saturated her senses, raising her blood pressure by several alarming degrees.

"Seven?" he repeated, watching her closely, wondering
when she'd back off. He nearly lost his balance when she
nodded.

"All right, seven."

She wasn't kidding. Bart couldn't think of a single witty
remark. "Fine, see you then." Turning, he walked to the
fence, gave Torey one last perplexed look, then clasped a
post and vaulted over the barbed wire.

Three

———

Three times in the next two hours Torey stood near the phone with the urge to call Bart and cancel the date. Whether he'd be anywhere near his phone was a moot point. Someone would answer...maybe one of the twins. Who would take the message wasn't the heart of Torey's concern; the thought of spending the evening with Bart Scanlon was driving her back to her childhood habit of biting her fingernails.

It had been so easy to get his attention, too easy, really. Torey didn't consider herself a particularly worldly woman, but neither was she naive, and she didn't have to waste a second's time on wondering what had been in Bart's mind during their little interchange. He was going to expect some hanky-panky this evening, and she'd encouraged the idea by flirting.

She had never been so indecisive. Excitement and dread battled within her with the force of a mini-tornado. Bart

Scanlon wasn't a man to play games with. His rugged exterior wasn't a facade. He was genuinely rough, tough and often crude.

Not that she had ever heard of Bart manhandling or forcing a woman into anything. Her suspicions were entirely based on her own feelings around the man. She'd always harbored a tiny bit of fear of Bart. He was too self-assured, too confident, not to be completely aware of his strength and unquestionable maleness.

When she told Lorna about the date Torey could see that the older woman was definitely taken aback. In a perfectly miserable tone of voice, Torey tried to explain what she, herself, didn't understand. "I just feel—I don't know, Lorna. Bart's very disturbing." She saw Lorna stare at her, then heave a sigh.

"Just be careful, Torey. Bart doesn't strike me as a man who'd be content with a platonic relationship for very long."

Torey couldn't disagree. "I know."

Lorna had prepared chicken and dumplings for dinner, a favorite dish of Torey's, but her stomach was so tight and achey it was an effort to eat. Halfway through the meal the telephone rang. Torey got up to answer the kitchen extension. "Lancaster Ranch."

"Torey? Steve. How are you?"

A stab of guilt made Torey wince. She and Steve had never even come close to discussing commitment, but she would bet her savings that Steve hadn't dated another woman since his move to Stanton. For that matter, Steve was the only man she'd been dating, too. Unlike Bart, Steve didn't have a demanding bone in his body. Their dates were pleasant events, movies, an occasional meal together, leisurely conversations and no pressure. It was what Torey had thought she wanted. Until recently.

"I'm fine, Steve. Having dinner. How are you?"

"You're eating? I won't keep you, then. But I'm going to be out your way this evening. Brock Mueller called and asked me to come by and check out a new foal. It shouldn't take long and I thought I'd stop by your place afterwards."

"Oh," Torey said very quietly, "I'm sorry, Steve, but I won't be here. I have...plans for this evening."

"Oh, I see. Well, in that case..."

Torey didn't know what else to say. She felt terrible. The last thing she would ever want to do was hurt a nice guy like Steve. She detected a falsely cheery note in Steve's next words.

"I'll give you a call in the next few days. Maybe we can get together this weekend."

"Yes," Torey agreed quickly. "Do call, Steve."

"I will. So long, Torey."

"Goodbye." Torey put the phone down and met Lorna's concerned brown eyes. "That was Steve," Torey said unnecessarily, returning to her place at the table.

"So I heard."

Torey covered her face with her hands and groaned. "What am I doing? Going out with Bart Scanlon is insane."

"Do you really feel that way?"

Dropping her hands, Torey frowned. "I don't know how I feel. That's the whole problem. I'll tell you something, Lorna. I'm actually praying that one evening with Bart will end this...this...I don't even know what to call it!"

"It might," Lorna said quietly. "And then again, it might result in the exact opposite. Torey, there's really nothing wrong with Bart. He's a hardworking man."

"He's got a reputation, Lorna. We both know that."

Lorna raised an eyebrow. "He's single, and I've never heard of him fooling around with a married woman, have you? I think that shows some regard for propriety."

Torey laughed humorlessly. "I doubt if Bart worries much about propriety."

"All right, morality, then. Or personal standard. Whatever, the women in Bart's life have all been unmarried and over twenty-one. Just like you, Torey. You're exercising free will by going out with him."

"And I'll have to accept the consequences, won't I?"

Lorna nodded solemnly. "I guess you will."

Nervous about such a naked truth, Torey got up and started to clear the table. Lorna stopped her. "You go and get ready. I'll do this."

"All right, thanks." It was getting close to seven, and Torey still hadn't decided what to wear, although she had bathed and done her hair before dinner. In her bedroom, she stood at the door of her closet and studied the neatly hung garments. Bart had mentioned having a drink, but a drink where? Montanans thought nothing of driving a hundred miles to reach a nice supper club or nightspot. But tomorrow was an ordinary workday, and Torey couldn't see Bart wanting to make a late night of it.

Casual was best in Montana in almost every case, and with Bart's personal clothing preference, Torey suspected that even a simple dress would be dressing up too much. Yet she fingered a creamy-colored sundress. It was almost new and very becoming, and she had even bought high-heeled sandals in the same buttery shade of rich cream. She had a shawl for her shoulders, which was a woven blend of cream, gray and taupe. The outfit was sure to bring an admiring glance from anyone who saw it.

Torey's heart palpitated at the thought of Bart's blue eyes washing over the ensemble. The sundress had narrow straps, exposing her arms, shoulders, and more than a hint of cleavage. He would stare, and not subtly, either. Knowing Bart, he might take it as an invitation.

No, that outfit was not for tonight. Tonight she would be well covered. Determinedly Torey reached for a pair of white slacks and a black-and-white patterned, short-sleeved top, which buttoned securely from a reasonably high neck to its bottom hem. White flats and a pair of black-and-white earrings completed the more sensible outfit, and after applying her makeup and giving herself a quick spritz of cologne, Torey was ready.

And just in time, she thought with an explosive panic at the sound of a vehicle outside. She studied herself in the mirror, noting the wild excitement in her eyes, and then her gaze moved down to her black-and-white clothing. She froze: This outfit wasn't Bart Scanlon, it was Steve Johnson!

Torey began ripping her clothes off, and she was yanking on a pair of stone-washed jeans when Lorna stuck her head in. "He's here."

"I know. Tell him I'll be out in five minutes." Dropping to her knees in the closet, Torey found her good lizard boots and pulled them on, then jumping up, she located her faded-denim shirt with the shoulder pads and brass buttons. The shirt was stylishly overlarge, and Torey belted it with a wide, low-slung lizard belt. Adding a tan Stetson, tipping it to a jaunty angle on her auburn curls, she drew a satisfied breath. *This* was Bart Scanlon.

She transferred lipstick, keys, hairbrush and wallet from the white bag she'd intended using to a large, soft, brown leather shoulder bag. Slinging it to her left shoulder, Torey took a final look in the mirror. She started from the room, then turned back and gave herself another spritz of cologne.

She bravely marched down the hall and into the living room. Bart was sitting on the couch, a pale gray Stetson in his hands, and he slowly got to his feet. He was shiny clean, wearing dark jeans, a white shirt and highly polished black boots. His hair had been trimmed, Torey realized, and was uncommonly subdued. It wasn't until she looked at his eyes did he even seem like the Bart she'd seen and talked to only a few hours ago. Within the radiance of that electric—yes, *electric*—blue was that note of mockery Torey was accustomed to, that hint of waiting she'd always interpreted as a readiness for an opportunity to cut her down.

He said nothing about her appearance, nor did she sense either approval or disapproval from him. "All set?" he asked.

"All set," she acknowledged, and turned to Lorna, who was occupying her favorite recliner chair with a strange expression. "I won't be late, Lorna."

"Have fun," Lorna said quietly.

Bart nodded at the older woman. "Good seeing you again, Lorna."

"Nice seeing you, too, Bart."

Torey led the way to the front door, so aware of Bart behind her she couldn't breathe normally. He reached around her and opened the door, and when she stepped out onto the porch she saw that Bart's black pickup had been washed and polished. It struck her that Bart had gone to quite a lot of trouble for this date, apparently driving to town to get a haircut, even cleaning his pickup.

He opened the driver's door. "Get in on this side."

"Thank you." Torey felt his hand on her arm for the climb up into the cab, and a starburst of tingles prickled her skin. She slid across the seat, almost to the opposite door. The interior of the pickup was clean, too, smelling of something lemony. Bart got in and closed the door, then turned on the key that he'd left in the ignition.

With the motor running, he gave her an unreadable look. "I really didn't think you'd come."

"I said I would." She wasn't looking at him, but she could feel his eyes on her.

"You look nice."

"So do you."

"Are you afraid to look at me?"

Torey turned her head slowly, and the impact of sitting in Bart Scanlon's pickup and really looking at him was like a sudden blow. Her breath caught in her throat. He was too handsome to be real. His coloring was incredible, dark skin, blue eyes, white teeth and black hair, eyebrows and lashes. Instead of blushing, Torey felt herself losing color. Whatever this crazy thing was that had suddenly warped her opinion of this man, it was pretty damned serious.

"I think I am," she admitted in a low strained voice.

Bart's eyes narrowed, and they stared at each other for a long time, with tension doubling and redoubling in the pickup. And then his hand left the steering wheel and moved toward her. Torey's gaze dropped to it, and it stopped within an inch of her arm.

"We better go," Bart muttered.

Torey took in some much needed air, realizing she'd been holding her breath. Her insides were churning with the sudden understanding that Bart now knew that something was very different between them. No, the difference was with her. She had changed, drastically.

The pickup reached the highway and turned south. Torey cleared her throat. "Where are we going?"

"I was thinking about Lottie's, but..."

Lottie's was a popular local saloon. "But...?" Torey questioned.

"Not Lottie's," Bart said emphatically, and shot her a quizzical look. What was going on with Torey Lancaster? She was sitting right beside him and he still found it hard to believe she hadn't backed out of the date. And that look they'd exchanged, and her admitting she was afraid to look at him—just what the hell *was* going on? He was game for anything she was, but this whole thing was weird.

"Maybe we'll just take a ride," he said under his breath.

"Pardon?"

"Nothing important. Any place special you'd like to go?"

"Well...no." Torey was still wondering why he'd changed his mind about Lottie's. It was a lively place and certainly good enough to have a drink at. A lot of the loggers and cattlemen in the area hung around Lottie's. "Lottie's is fine, Bart. Really."

"No," he said brusquely, and swung his eyes from the road to her in a rather hard glance. Torey swallowed nervously, realizing that he didn't want to take her to Lottie's. Didn't she look good enough? she wondered, wishing that she hadn't changed from the black-and-white outfit. There were bound to be people at Lottie's that they both knew, and maybe he thought she looked too cowgirlish, too kicky, too something or other.

It came to Torey then that they didn't have even one subject in common to talk about. Cutting to the bottom line, and despite having lived as neighbors most of their lives, they weren't familiar enough with each other to even know if they had any common interests. She wilted internally. This was a mistake, a terrible, unholy mistake. She felt like a total idiot, like a tongue-tied girl on her first date. And Bart wasn't helping any; he was acting like he didn't know what to say, either.

She couldn't stand the heavy silence. "We've sure been having great weather lately," she commented brightly.

He took his eyes off the road and looked at her again. "Why'd you agree to this?"

She should have known Bart wouldn't beat around the bush. Actually, she had known it. It was one of the points she'd worried about earlier today, fretting that if he really was crude enough to bring up the question, she would feel like a nitwit. Well, he was and she did.

But it was an intolerable sensation, and Torey steeled herself for a round of Bart's caustic wit. "Why did you ask for this?" she retorted.

In profile again, she saw him grin faintly. "I'm not sure it was my idea."

"Oh? Well, if you prefer to call it off, just turn around and take me back home."

"Is that what you want me to do?"

"Is that what you want to do?"

He threw her a scorching, daring look. "Want me to show you what *I* want?"

Torey's pulse went wild. He'd show her what he wanted if she even blinked funny. But show her how? Would he stop the pickup right here on the highway and make love to her if she said yes? And if it came to that, would he hurry or go slow? Was he a tender lover or was he rough and demanding? Which of all the multitude of possibilities would she prefer? What were Bart Scanlon's kisses like? What did he taste like, feel like?

What if she led him into a kiss and then decided she didn't like it? Would he stop if she told him to?

"You sure are thinking hard. Tough question, huh?" he drawled, fully expecting her to screech at him like she'd always done in the past when he'd gone too far with his teasing.

"I just haven't decided on the answer yet."

Bart laughed, but it wasn't one of his full-of-confidence-that-he'd-gotten-to-her laughs. Torey was still surprising him, and it was such a deviation from what he was used to from her, he wasn't sure how to react. Still, it wasn't like him to let a woman get the last word. "Well, you just let me know when you do decide, honey. I'll be real glad to find a nice, secluded parking spot."

Torey didn't immediately shoot back a reply. Bandying words about sex, which was what this was really all about, was strangely exhilarating. Maybe she *could* handle Bart Scanlon. "Fine," she agreed coolly.

Bart had never had any trouble recognizing a challenge from a woman, and if Torey Lancaster wasn't issuing one, he'd eat his hat. He gave up on figuring out why and decided to just go along with it. The evening promised to be even more intriguing than he'd previously thought. This ordinarily straitlaced, antagonistic woman was coming on to him, and if that's what she wanted from him, he'd be more than glad to comply.

The atmosphere was getting shadowy as the sun dropped behind the mountains. Bart switched on the radio, giving Torey a quick glance. "What do you like?"

"Pardon?"

"What kind of music?"

The radio was already tuned to a country station. "That's fine," she told him. "I like any kind of music, other than hard rock."

Bart nodded.

"Apparently you like country best."

He shrugged. "I'm not really into music. Don't have time for it."

The information didn't surprise Torey. Running a ranch was in itself time-consuming, but Bart was also logging his mountain and constructing a road. *And,* Torey added with a stinging sarcasm, *let's not forget that he's also keeping several ladies in the area happy.*

She frowned. Just how much truth was there in that final observation? It was based on gossip, of course. Over the years Torey had seen Bart with a few different women, but the man had a right to female companionship. It was just that now that she'd recognized Bart's considerable charms, placing him as ardent lover to those women was oddly unnerving.

He was an intriguing man, Torey decided. That's what this was all about. For some reason she had suddenly started responding to Bart's dark and moody aura. Was it because Steve's kisses were only blandly exciting? Or could it be because she was twenty-eight years old and realizing that she had thus far lived a remarkably unexciting life?

When had she ever had sweaty palms from just being in the same vehicle with a man? When had she ever felt breathless and slightly choked because a man's hands looked sexy on a steering wheel?

Bart's did. He had long slender fingers with square nails. The cuffs of his white shirt were buttoned around his strong wrists, a large sturdy watch adorning the left one, the only jewelry in sight. Torey recalled the sleeveless shirts she'd seen him in, and how the bronzed skin of his arms had rippled from the muscles beneath it, and absentmindedly she dried her damp palms on the legs of her jeans.

They reached the outskirts of Stanton and Bart slowed the pickup's speed way down. Halfway through town he veered the truck to the curb and stopped, cutting the engine. "Wait here. I'll only be a minute."

Torey watched him amble into the liquor store, gnawing her bottom lip with some trepidation. She'd never heard that Bart was a drinker, but then she didn't usually encourage friends to gossip. Maybe that was one item that had escaped her.

She was relieved when he came out with only one small bottle of wine and a package of plastic glasses. Bart placed his purchases on the seat and got back behind the wheel. He gave her a lazy grin. "Hope you like Cabernet."

Torey smiled, if a little weakly, much more concerned with where he intended to drink the wine than what kind it was. She'd wanted to get to know Bart better, but just how much better? Was she really ready for an isolated parking spot and a bottle of wine?

When he made a U-turn, drove back through town and then took a left onto Foothills Road, Torey knew where he was going. Indian Leap overlooked the entire valley, offering a spectacular view. But not at night, and Bart had turned the headlights on. He wasn't driving clear to Indian Leap just to stare at the less than memorable lights of Stanton.

She'd asked for this. Anything that Bart decided to try, she had definitely asked for. Her about-face had been too abrupt. He had to have gotten some very erotic ideas from it.

Maybe she should set him straight right now, before they reached the summit. Torey's hands clenched and unclenched nervously. A distinctly recognizable voice came from the radio, singing his latest hit song. The pickup's motor churned behind the music, Torey's heartbeat echoed in her own ears, and the tension in the cab of the truck kept increasing.

This had to be the most uncommunicative date she'd ever been a part of. Bart didn't even attempt conversation, and everything she thought of to say seemed trite or childish or both. They had nothing to talk about, not one thing. Why was she here?

And why didn't she just tell him to turn around!

The headlights caught several deer feeding at the side of the road, and Bart slowed down. "One of them is a fawn," he said quietly, and Torey craned her neck to see the smaller animal.

"Do you hunt?" she asked, then winced at the inane question. Of course he hunted. Bart Scanlon was the consummate Montana male, full of the outdoors and his command of it.

"I hunt," he confirmed. "Do you?"

The question wasn't out of line; there were women in the area who enjoyed hunting as much as their husbands and brothers did. "No," Torey admitted, somehow feeling inadequate because of her repugnance for killing beautiful animals, wishing she'd never brought up the subject.

"There's a lot you don't do, isn't there?"

She almost felt relieved at the teasing note in his voice. It was familiar, at least. Choking on sexual tension wasn't. "That's probably a matter of opinion," she replied stiffly. "I'm satisfied with my life-style."

"I've met your boyfriend, you know. Steve what's-his-name."

"Johnson. Steve Johnson. And he's not my boyfriend."

"Lover? Fiancé?"

Torey swallowed the quick anger she felt. Bart was baiting her, and she was falling into his old trap. "Steve is a good friend."

Bart hooted. "A good friend? Is that how he sees you, too, as a good friend?"

"I'm sure he does."

"Then he must be a real exciting date," Bart drawled sardonically. "What do you do, sit around and watch old reruns on TV?" He chuckled, as if savoring the image.

His overbearing attitude infuriated Torey. "Do you think this date is so exciting? Riding around in a pickup is hardly something to put in one's diary, Scanlon."

He grinned wickedly. "The evening's not over yet, honey. You might have something real interesting to write about before we say good night."

Torey's stomach turned over. Handle Bart? That idea had to be the most senseless she'd ever had! She was getting in way, way over her head. They hadn't met a car in miles and were getting farther away from lights and people with each passing minute. Unless another couple had decided to spend the evening at Indian Leap, they would be extremely isolated up there. She would literally be at Bart Scanlon's mercy, and she didn't even know if he had any.

She took a ragged breath. "I've changed my mind. Take me home."

Bart had been expecting that, but they were almost to Indian Leap and he was going to find out just what had prompted this strange evening before taking Torey home, whether she liked it or not. "Coward," he accused softly.

"Call me anything you like, but take me home. I'm sorry I led you to think . . ."

"What, Torey? What did you lead me to think?"

Her face was flaming, probably bright enough to see in the dark, she thought. Bart was too much for her to deal with, too direct, too . . .

"That you need a man?"

Oh, Lord. He was even worse than she'd thought. Torey squeezed her eyes shut, wishing she was anywhere but here, trapped in this insufferable man's pickup, in the mountains, in the dark. "You're so crude I can't believe it," she whispered.

"Crude? Or honest. Did you just discover sex, honey? For your information, it's been around a long, long time."

"Stop it, Bart."

"Tell me something. How does a gal with your maidenly outlook deal with the realities of ranch life? Do you look the other way when a bull mounts a heifer?"

"Don't relate the natural process of animal procreation to the intricacies of human relationships! There's no comparison, and no, I'm not so delicate that I have to look the other way when a bull—" He was laughing! Thoroughly enjoying her outburst. Torey clamped her mouth shut and glared out the side window. "You're impossible," she fumed angrily.

"And you're the cutest thing in three counties. Why do you get so mad when I tease you? Hasn't it ever occurred to you that that's the very reason I do it? When we were kids, you puffed up like a little toad. You stamped your foot and screamed at me, and I loved it. I couldn't wait to yank your hair ribbons loose or grab your lunch pail again.''

"You were an insufferable brat!"

"I was sweet on you."

Torey's mouth dropped open. "You were what?"

"You were the only girl on the bus with long curls. As young as I was, I wanted to stick my finger in those curls and see what they felt like. I'd sit behind you and stare at those damned curls until I couldn't stand it anymore, then I'd go for your ribbons." Bart laughed softly. "Funny, huh?"

Funny? Torey smiled weakly. It really wasn't very funny at all. She'd never suspected that Bart's aggravating attentions had been because of a kid's crush. He'd been her nemesis, a cross to bear, a reason to be glad the few times she'd caught a cold or the flu and had to miss school.

She wondered about high school and if he had still secretly liked her. She didn't find out, because they had reached Indian Leap and Bart was pulling to a stop at the very edge of the overlook. He turned off the motor and rolled his window down. A quick check of the area evidenced their solitude: No one else had chosen this spot to be alone at tonight.

She was completely on her own. With Bart Scanlon and a bottle of wine.

Four

The wine bottle had a twist-off cap. Bart opened it and filled one of the plastic glasses about half-full. He held it out. "Here, have a little wine."

Torey hesitated. Accepting the wine would be an agreement to participate in Bart's idea of a date. This was a romantic spot. A high breeze was rustling the tops of the dense stand of tall pine trees surrounding the viewpoint and crickets were singing their nocturnal mating call. The night air coming through Bart's opened window was cool and smelled of rich, moist greenery, trees, brush, moss. It was an ideal setting for lovers, for two people who wanted to escape the trappings of so-called civilized dating and get off by themselves.

Was there a message in Bart's decision to forego Lottie's boisterous activity for this?

Sighing softly, unsure of her ability to read *any* of Bart's messages, Torey took the glass and watched him fill another. He recapped the bottle and balanced it upright against the steering column. "Here's looking at you, kid," he said, doing a bad imitation of Humphrey Bogart's famous line, bringing a genuine laugh to Torey's lips, certainly the first of the evening. She took a sip of wine and lowered the glass, wondering what would come next.

"Do you know why this is called Indian Leap?" Bart murmured.

"Yes. A beautiful Indian girl, the daughter of a chief, leaped to her death because of the loss of her lover." Everyone knew the old legend, although no one knew if it was really true.

"That would take a powerful kind of love, don't you think?"

"Or a trace of insanity," Torey quipped. "The rest of the story says that her lover only married another woman, hardly a reason to leap into oblivion."

"Obviously you're not very romantic."

"And you are?" Torey drawled skeptically. Bart Scanlon, romantic? No way. He was sexy as all get out, but he had never struck her as the romantic type. Expecting a snappy comeback, Torey was surprised to hear a rather doleful sigh.

"I guess I'm not. But I might be, with the right woman."

That stopped her for a minute. She certainly hadn't anticipated that kind of vulnerable remark from Bart Scanlon. Silently she took another swallow of wine.

"Apparently you haven't met the right man, either," Bart said quietly.

"Apparently not."

"Do you want to get married?"

"What?"

Bart roared with laughter. "That wasn't a proposal, honey. I only meant do you want to get married *someday?*"

Self-deprecating laughter was Torey's only defense against the blistering embarrassment she was suffering. For a second there, she really had thought Bart had proposed. "I thought that was rather sudden. You scared the breath out of me."

"I haven't even kissed you. A man certainly wouldn't propose to a woman he hasn't kissed," Bart teased.

"Of course not." Torey had answered quickly, but her senses had automatically responded to the suggestiveness in Bart's teasing. She really did want him to kiss her, if he'd stop at a kiss. She honestly didn't know if he would or wouldn't. Bart exuded the smell of danger, along with a spicy, sexy scent that she thought was after-shave.

He laughed then, a low, seductive sound. "I used to wonder what kissing you would be like. Hell, I wondered about a lot more than just kissing you. In high school, a guy's thoughts go a lot further than kissing."

Torey cleared her throat. So he *had* liked her in high school. It was stupefying news to her. "You found out, didn't you? What kissing me was like, I mean."

"And nearly got my head knocked off in the process." Bart chuckled. Then he sobered. "Yeah, I found out, but I also found out that you wanted no part of Bart Scanlon. I guess I'd always known it, but it didn't sink in until that kiss." He turned in the seat, facing her, stretching his arm along the top of the seatback. "So what is this really all about, Torey? I'm serious this time. You've brought back a lot of old urges, and I'd like to know why?"

She sat perfectly still, afraid that if she moved she would brush against the hand she felt directly behind her head. "I didn't know you thought of me...in that way," she said uneasily.

"Which only makes tonight even more of a mystery," he said softly.

"Do we *have* to talk about it?"

He was silent a moment. "No, not if you don't want to." He touched her hair then, and a sublime sensation washed over Torey. She closed her eyes as his fingers gently twisted curls. "It feels exactly like I thought it would, silky and soft. Why are you trembling? Do I frighten you?"

She nodded. "Then why are you out with me?" he demanded harshly. "I'm not a kid, Torey." Abruptly Bart placed the glass he'd been holding in his left hand on the dash. He took hers away from her and set it up there, too. "You're not a kid, either," he said huskily, and took her chin, bringing her face around. "Are you going to try to sock me again after I kiss you?"

"No," she whispered, moistening her lips with her tongue.

Bart watched the process, then brought his face down and ran the tip of his tongue across her lips. Torey gasped as an electric current shot through her. That wasn't kissing! That was...

She couldn't even label the most sensual thing a man had ever done to her. "Bart," she breathed unsteadily.

"Bart, yes, or Bart, no?" he whispered.

"I..."

"Don't you know?"

"Would...would a kiss satisfy you?" she whispered.

"Would a kiss satisfy you? Maybe we should find out." His mouth brushed hers, then settled firmly upon it. Every cell in Torey's body slumped with an overwhelming weakness. Bart Scanlon's mouth on hers was like nothing she had ever experienced. It tasted like wine and moved sensuously, a gentle teaser that was stealing her breath and doing crazy things to her body.

His lips parted, and his tongue moved lazily into her mouth, exploring the moist contours within. Torey kept getting weaker. There was a flame devouring her insides, and her muscles kept losing strength. She lifted one of her hands to his chest and contact with a hard wall of male flesh beneath the crisp white cotton of his shirt sent a whole new upheaval of emotions rocketing through her.

His hands were still above her shoulders, one in her hair, the other caressing her face. She heard the unevenness of his breathing and felt the heat of his body. His mouth raised from hers by a fraction. "That's some chemistry, honey," he whispered raggedly. "But I can't say I'm satisfied, can you?"

Torey tried to search his eyes in the dark, looking for just what she didn't know. While she wasn't a virgin, she'd never taken sex lightly, and she strongly suspected that Bart did. But that's where the kind of emotion storming her was leading. Satisfied? No, she was far from satisfied. A yearning of monstrous proportions was tearing her apart. Her breasts ached, and flames licked at and tormented her lower body.

"You're... very experienced at this, aren't you?" she questioned.

"Want me to lie about it?"

"No, no lies, please."

"And you're not, are you?"

"Not very."

He trailed his forefinger slowly downward, caressing her cheek, her throat, then the blue shirt to the tip of a breast. Torey sucked in a sharp breath, but she didn't stop him from rolling her nipple between his thumb and fingers. "Nice," he murmured. "Very nice. You're a beautiful woman, Torey Lancaster."

"Am I?"

He began unbuttoning the brass buttons on her shirt, slowly, unhurriedly. Mesmerized, she did nothing to stop him. She wanted him to go on and on....

And on?

This was a first date, for crying out loud! They hardly knew one another. Being long-time neighbors had no meaning, not when avoidance had been the keynote of their strange relationship.

Torey grabbed his hand. "No, wait!"

He pressed his mouth into the soft undercurve of her jaw. "Wait for what? We both know what we want."

She shuddered at the delicious, rippling sensation of his lips nibbling at her throat. "One kiss, Bart. That's all we've shared. It's not enough for..."

"Fine. I enjoy the kissing almost as much as I'll enjoy the rest of it." He sought her lips again.

She jerked her head around. "That's not what I meant!"

He sat up. "All right, what *did* you mean? Honey, you kissed me back like a woman who knows exactly what she wants. I was only taking my cue from you."

Honesty beat in Torey's brain. Was there anything wrong with telling him the truth? Would he accept anything less? She drew a deep breath. "I don't like lies and evasions," she began. "So, yes, I do know what I want. But I don't always give in to my whims, Bart."

"Oh, so I'm a whim?"

"You're..." Torey closed her eyes for a moment. "You're something I can't explain. You're a... dark...magnet. If that sounds crazy to you, just triple it for what it sounds like to me."

"And this crazy feeling just came over you all of a sudden?"

He was making fun of her now. She could hear the bemusement in his voice. "I'm always so entertaining to you, aren't I?"

He smiled. "More so than ever, now that I know what's going on behind those innocent-looking gray eyes. So, Torey really is torrid. Under that cool exterior beats the heart of a passionate woman. Interesting, honey, real interesting.''

Torey finished rebuttoning the two brass buttons he'd undone. "I really don't like you," she said quietly, stung from his offhanded cynicism. "You never were likable, and it's evident you haven't changed."

"But *you* have. You don't like me and yet here you are, drawn to my 'dark magnetism.'"

He'd pronounced "dark magnetism" in a particularly demeaning way, stabbing Torey to the quick. He was more than making fun of her now, he was digging at raw nerves. "Please take me home," she demanded.

Her tone riled Bart. "You know, I think you're expecting me to say, 'Put out or walk home.' Are you, Torey? Is that what's in the back of your devious little mind? Maybe you'd like me to use a little force. That way you could have your fun without any responsibility for a decision. Honey, you're burning for me. I'll be damned if I know what caused it after all these years, but there's not a modicum of doubt in my mind about it."

Torey's eyes flashed angrily. "Some gentleman you are!"

"Gentleman!" Bart whooped. "Lady, if that's what you're looking for, you're barking up the wrong tree."

"Which I already knew. I'll tell you something, Bart. Sometimes people do foolish things—" Torey's words stopped in a torrent of emotion. Bart had yanked her into a viselike embrace. She was up against his chest, held fast with hard, hot muscles. "What're you doing?"

"Just showing you what you're missing, honey." His mouth came down on hers hard, with none of the gentleness he'd kissed her with before. He'd really thought she would capitulate, that she'd end up whimpering and wanting more, like she had before. But she only squirmed and struggled and shouted wordless fury deep in her throat. He kissed her until he was ready to stop kissing her, and then he let her go, as abruptly as he'd grabbed her.

Torey's mouth felt bruised and swollen. "You insufferable jerk," she said hoarsely.

"Sorry. That didn't prove a thing, did it?" Bart slid across the seat and started the truck, angry that he'd let Torey Lancaster get to him. At the last second before putting the pickup in reverse to back up and turn around, he remembered the two glasses of wine on the dash. Snatching them up, he tossed them out the window.

Torey glared. "On top of everything else, you're a litterbug."

"Dry up!" Slamming the truck in reverse, Bart gunned the motor and backed up fast. Then he slammed the shifting lever again and the pickup shot forward.

Torey fastened her seat belt. "This road is treacherous in the dark. I'd appreciate some concern for my safety, even if you don't care about yours."

"You know what you are, Torey? A damned tease. Why me? If you had to suddenly develop a libido, why in hell pick on me?"

Why, indeed. Sick at heart, Torey stared into the black trees on her side of the truck, wishing she had a ready answer to the question. Well, was she cured of that idiotic urge to sample Bart Scanlon?

Yes, she told herself vehemently. She most certainly *was* cured. She might not feel better right at this moment, but she would. Tomorrow morning when she woke up. Bart would be notably absent from her system. And what a welcome relief that would be!

They rode in silence, but Torey sensed Bart's simmering anger. She told herself to ignore it, that Bart *always* simmered, for one reason or another. But as they reached the highway, she had the craziest urge to slide across the seat and curl up against him, to tell him not to be angry, to *soothe* him.

It was a preposterous idea. Soothing Bart Scanlon would be like baiting a grizzly. He might take the bait, but then one would have a wild bear on her hands. No, it was best to leave Bart completely alone, which, Lord help her, Torey wished she had done. Her instincts had been sound years ago, and she should have continued to heed their warnings.

On the highway, Bart drove fast. Not recklessly, but faster than the speed limit. He probably always did, Torey thought with an uneasy glance at the speedometer. They were basically different kinds of people. She abided by and respected law and order in every situation, even if the local law was a dunce like Roscoe Ledbetter. She never exceeded the speed limit and she wouldn't litter for love or money. Bart was a maverick, living by his own rules. The world was lucky that he wasn't criminally inclined because he seemed to wear danger like a halo.

Or, was she the only one who felt like that?

No, Lorna, too, sensed that Bart wasn't anyone to fool with. Maybe women sensed that in Bart. Maybe women were *drawn* to that in Bart.

Well, thank goodness she was over that bit of female idiocy. Torey frowned. She *was* over it, wasn't she?

Bart pulled off of the highway onto her quarter-mile driveway. But instead of speeding to her front door, he stopped the pickup immediately after the turn. Torey looked at him expectantly. "Now what?"

"I want to say something. I've been thinking, and my first impulse was to tell you that the next time you get a hankering to play with the big boys, go and find some other fool. But I've changed my mind about that. I think you're what they call a late bloomer, honey, and you're getting tired of mush when you could have steak."

Stunned, Torey merely stared.

"Anyway, that hankering isn't going to go away on its own. You might still be able to control your whims, but that noble trait won't satisfy that itch you've got for very long. Just so you know, I'd like to be the man to make a real woman out of you. I'll be around, and you sure know where I live."

Speech escaped Torey. Her mind wasn't even working very well. Never had a man talked to her in such an insulting, debasing way, and her reaction was a shocked shutdown of her normal faculties. She watched Bart start the pickup moving again, wearing a sardonic half-smile, sending her piercing little glances, and humiliation kept her nearly numb.

And then her eyes began to burn. Facing front, Torey blinked hard and fast to keep the tears back. Hatred of enormous magnitude sprouted in the pit of her stomach and spread throughout her body, and right behind it, anger, fury. They were almost to the house when she began to speak.

"You arrogant, egotistical jerk," she said in a voice shaking with emotion. "If a woman had the slightest inclination to hope for anything from you, you would find a way to destroy it. Your clever remarks, your despicable, perverted sense of humor, your overbearing confidence that Bart Scanlon is the greatest thing walking around on two feet would do it even without your intolerable crudity."

"Hey, you don't need to get so ticked off!"

"Ticked off? I'm furious, *not* ticked off. You're disgusting."

This wasn't fun or funny, and he'd thought it would be. He'd meant to shock her and let her know, at the same time, that he wasn't really mad because she'd teased and backed down. He felt anger rising, too, defensive anger. Who was prim, proper Torey Lancaster to label him disgusting just because he called a spade a spade? He could have talked a hell of a lot plainer than he had, as a matter of fact.

"Stuff it, Torey," he said coldly, weary of the game. "Maybe your current boyfriend enjoys your lack of humor and cold-fish attitude, but I don't."

"Oh, pardon me for wounding your delicate sensibilities. But if you were trying to be funny with those vile remarks, you missed the mark by a mile!"

"Vile remarks? You're a sad case, lady, a frustrated old maid who's afraid to live." Bart stopped the truck, glad to have finally reached her house. "I don't suppose you want me to walk you to the door, so good night."

"And good riddance!" she yelled, livid from that "old maid" insult. Why was it that an unmarried woman of twenty-eight was called an old maid, while a single man of thirty was a bachelor? The disparity in terms was maddening.

Climbing out her side of the pickup, Torey left the door hanging open and ran for the house. Bart watched her go with a disgusted expression, then impatiently slid across the seat and yanked the door closed, muttering, "Damned woman."

Before he drove away, although there was little chance of Torey hearing him from inside the house, he yelled out the window, "You're a dried-up old maid, and I pity Steve what's-his-name, the poor sap!"

Five

Torey heard Bart's parting shot very well. It set her hair on end and tensed every muscle in her body. If it took twenty years she would pay him back, she thought with rigid fury. There had to be a way, and she would find it if she had to dedicate her life to that goal!

Then, fuming and suddenly trembling, a nerve-wracking combination that brought tears to Torey's eyes, she snapped off the living-room lamp Lorna had left burning and started feeling her way to her room in the dark. She tried to move quietly so she wouldn't wake Lorna, more for herself than for Lorna. Torey felt in no condition to answer even a simple, "Did you have a nice time?"

A nice time. The very term grated and created another gush of tears. Yes, there was some self-pity mingling with all of the anger and murderous impulses crashing around in her brain. But who wouldn't feel sorry for themselves after a clash with Bart Scanlon? As dates went, tonight had

been a complete disaster. After this, a quiet evening with
Steve would be a delight.

Gaining her bedroom, Torey silently closed the door and
started undressing without a light. She dropped her clothes
in a heap, fished a nightgown out of a dresser drawer,
yanked it on and crawled into bed. Angrily she brushed at
the tears still seeping from her eyes. Why was she crying?
Only an idiot would cry over Bart Scanlon.

The tears kept flowing, prompting Torey to make an ir-
rational wish: If there was only some way to make *him* cry!
It was a ludicrous hope, really. Men like Bart Scanlon
didn't cry; they made other people cry. Why had she been
so foolhardy? It wasn't as if she hadn't known how cruel
Bart could be.

She wasn't going to wake up in the morning cleansed of
those unholy cravings, either. Just thinking of Bart's kisses
started up all sorts of reactions. What's more, she couldn't
stop herself from imagining more than kisses, even while
lying there hating him and hoping that a flash of inspira-
tion would suddenly show her a way to get even with him.

Just once, if she could best Bart Scanlon just one time...

Torey sighed. She might as well forget that. What could
she ever do to bring him down a peg or two? The man was
as hard as nails, with a skin two inches thick. Anything she
said to him, he gave back to her double. "Go to sleep," she
commanded herself grumpily.

As Torey had expected, the morning sun didn't mean relief. She awoke with a dull headache and a bad taste in her
mouth, both afflictions caused by a stupid dream in which
Bart Scanlon had annoyingly played a starring role. After
the fiasco of last night's date, it didn't surprise Torey that
Bart had invaded her dreams. But wouldn't he die laughing if he ever heard about it?

Not that he would. After those crude, insulting remarks last night, it would be a cold day in hell before she even gave Bart Scanlon the time of day again, let alone confess he'd been in her dreams!

Lorna was an early riser and had the coffee perking and breakfast started when Torey walked into the kitchen. "Take a look at the next step in Bart Scanlon's road project," the older woman said.

Torey went outside. The air was cool and fresh, and the grass was dewy. But the morning's lovely serenity was destroyed by the sight of a second huge machine on the other side of the fence line. It was a grader, and three men—one of them Bart—were standing together, talking. The big tractor was some distance away, silent yet, apparently awaiting its operator. Torey had been aware of its progress toward the mountain. Daily, the huge machine had gradually pulled away from the vicinity of her house and outbuildings, a welcome reprieve from noise and dust.

But obviously the grader and another operator had arrived to begin working. After that, according to what Bart had said, the gravel trucks would be along. Once the gravel was down, the road would be usable and logging trucks would be going back and forth regularly. It wasn't a pleasant prospect.

Would poplars help? Would *anything* she could do help?

Disgusted, Torey started to turn back to the house. But just then she saw Bart break away from the other two men. As he changed positions he saw her, and he raised his hand in a wave that struck Torey as uniquely Bart Scanlon. How he could put his entire overbearing, conceited personality into one brief gesture, she would never know. But she instantly knew that he thought she'd been watching because of him!

"Stuff it, Scanlon," she muttered, and darted through the back door, stifling an urge to show *him* a gesture or two.

Lorna was pouring coffee. "Bart doesn't waste much time, does he?"

"He goes right for the gusto," Torey replied sourly.

"What?"

Torey's face reddened. Lorna had been talking about Bart and the road, while *she* had been talking about Bart and a much more painful topic.

"Didn't you two get along last night?" Lorna asked dryly, apparently catching on to Torey's mood.

Torey plopped down at the table and reached for her glass of orange juice. "No one could get along with Bart for more than five minutes. He's the most impossibly rude individual I've ever been around."

"Oh, really?" Lorna took her place at the table. "I wonder how he acquired such a fast reputation with the ladies, in that case," she said musingly.

Torey nearly choked on a mouthful of orange juice. Lorna appeared not to notice and went on talking. "I mean, if he's that rude, one has to wonder how he ever gets a second date. A first one is completely understandable. Bart's a handsome man. But one evening of rudeness is usually enough for most women."

Torey couldn't tell if Lorna was teasing or not. There was a sort of tongue-in-cheek quality to her tone. "You're not quite taking me seriously, are you?" Torey asked suspiciously.

Laughing, Lorna reached across the table and patted Torey's hand. "Let me put it this way, Torey. If you had said this morning that the evening with Bart had been boring, I would have known he was a lost cause. But he riled the female in you, didn't he?"

"He riled something, I don't mind admitting."

Lorna picked up the cereal box and sprinkled corn flakes into her bowl. "There's an old saying: Fighting cats have kittens."

Torey's eyes widened. "Bart Scanlon and I are not going to have kittens!"

"He's a sexy guy, Torey. Last night, when you came into the living room, even I could feel the electricity between you two."

"That's not true!"

Lorna shrugged. "I only call it as I see it. Here, have some cereal." Lorna shoved the box across the table.

Bart got home after dark that night. He was bone tired, dirty and hungry enough to eat anything that wasn't moving too fast to catch. The twins were sprawled in front of the TV in the living room, tired, too, Bart knew. Rob and Rich worked at the logging site, doing whatever job needed doing that day. They were good workers and were putting most of their pay in the bank for their education.

"Did you guys eat?" Bart asked wearily.

"We fried some hamburgers. There's meat left in the refrigerator," Rich volunteered. "Want me to cook it for you, Bart?"

"Would you mind? I'm really beat tonight."

Rich uncoiled his six feet of lanky body from the couch. "I'll do it while you shower."

"Thanks." As Bart headed for the bathroom, he heard the radio come on in the kitchen. The mixture of sounds blaring from the television set and the radio made Bart's head ache, but he ignored it, as he always did. The twins thrived on music and noise, while he was enjoying peace and quiet more and more. He must be getting old, he thought as he began stripping.

The bathroom was a mess, as usual. Wet towels were draped over the top of the shower and the two wall rods, with one lying in a soggy heap on the counter. Shaving gear, toothpaste, an array of cans, bottles and tubes of toiletries were scattered everywhere Bart looked. The sink was dirty, the toilet was dirty, the shower was dirty. The whole house was a sty, which was pretty damned disheartening to come home to night after night.

Every so often Bart would roust the boys into a cleaning spree. All three of them would shake and wash scatter rugs, sweep, vacuum and scrub floors, catch up on the mountain of laundry that seemed to pile up with the speed of light, wash dishes and sticky pans, clean the whole place from top to bottom.

But it never lasted. The Scanlon men were too busy trying to make enough money to pay for two upcoming medical educations to worry about a clean house. They dropped clothes, newspapers and magazines wherever they happened to be when they were through with them; they only did the dishes when there weren't any clean ones left in the cabinets; and the dirty laundry was a constant source of irritation.

Bart knew they needed a housekeeper. They'd *always* needed a housekeeper, ever since he came home from college and took over the job of raising his brothers. But it hadn't been that apparent before he began the logging project. He'd had more time to keep the house up and cook something decent to eat with only the ranch to run. He was a fair cook when he put his mind to it, and he even liked doing it.

But it had been quite a while since he'd had the time to cook or clean or do much of anything but work. Last night had been an exception he hadn't been able to pass up. A date with Torey Lancaster, one she had practically come right out and asked for had been impossible to forego.

And it had been a complete flop.

Grimacing at the memory, Bart turned the shower water on and stepped into the stall. The hot water felt good, reviving, and he vigorously shampooed his hair and soaped his body.

All day long Torey had been in the back of his mind, sometimes bursting to the forefront of his thoughts and delivering a wallop where it was bound to bother him the most. In spite of a close to puritan morality, the woman conveyed an inner sensuality that wouldn't stop bugging him. Bart wondered if Torey even knew the effect she had on him. She sure hadn't known it years ago. From what he'd gathered last night, it had never occurred to her that he might have been tormenting her because he liked her.

Did he like her now? That really was the sixty-four-dollar question. She stirred him up, he had no doubt about that. But like her?

Well, maybe he did. He'd always gotten a little silly whenever they ran into each other, and maybe he'd even regressed a little to that lovesick boy he'd been so many years ago. But he didn't know how to just talk to Torey, although he had no trouble talking to other women.

Maybe the date would have gone better if he'd taken her to Lottie's, as he'd originally planned. But after seeing how beautiful Torey looked, he hadn't wanted to take her to a place where ninety percent of the patrons were hard-talking men. Lottie's wasn't good enough for Torey Lancaster.

But neither was a bottle of inexpensive wine and Indian Leap, Bart reminded himself, wincing at how badly the evening had turned out.

Slamming the shower off, Bart shook the wet hair out of his face and reached for a towel. What had gnawed at him all day was whether or not he should make another attempt with Torey. He still didn't know the answer.

Walking out of the bathroom stark naked, Bart went to his bedroom and found a pair of clean jeans. The smell of frying hamburger wafting through the house made his mouth water, and he hurried to the kitchen to eat.

* * *

On Saturday morning Torey walked the fence line. The tractor and grader were parked and silent for the weekend, and Torey was trying to figure out if it was best to put in those poplars and completely block the view, or keep the view and put up with the dust and dirt of Bart's logging trucks. Nothing would block the noise, but the trees, if planted densely enough, would screen an awful lot of the dust.

There would be no point to tackling the job unless she insisted on large, mature trees and lots of them, Torey decided. Many ranchers used a row of poplars for a windbreak, so she knew they were effective, besides being attractive. It boiled down to whether she preferred looking at trees or dividing the view between big ugly logging trucks and the Montana countryside. Lorna had voted for the trees, but Torey knew that she would have to make the final decision.

Stepping off the area paralleling the house, Torey counted and came up with twenty-two trees. At fifty dollars a tree—she had already talked to a local supplier—the cost would be eleven hundred dollars. Bart's half would be five hundred and fifty bucks, and that wasn't even considering the cost of putting them in. Would he go that high? She could get poplars for much less, of course, but they were too small to be of any use this summer.

Pondering the problem, Torey turned at the sound of an approaching vehicle. It was Bart's black pickup, she saw with a strange flip of her stomach, and actually thought of running for the house. Since their ridiculous date, they hadn't been close enough to each other to speak, and Torey would just as soon keep it that way.

However, letting Bart think she was afraid of him was intolerable. She might be trapped at the fence, but she was on her own land, and if he dared to start something she was going to let him have it with both barrels.

The pickup rolled and bumped over the still primitive roadbed and came to a stop just across the fence from Torey. Bart got out. He was bareheaded and wearing dark glasses. His blue chambray shirt was unbuttoned as it usually was, three buttons down, and his soft, threadbare jeans fit like a second skin.

Torey refused to look at the dark hair visible in the V of Bart's half-open shirt. "Good morning," she said coolly.

Bart grinned. "Mending fences this morning? Maybe I came along at just the right time."

"My fences are in perfect condition."

"*All* of them?"

"If you're referring to you and me—" Torey broke off, realizing Bart was already getting her goat. She wasn't going to bandy words with him any more, she vowed again. "I was attempting to make a sensible decision about the poplars."

Bart's grin broadened. "You do have trouble with decisions, don't you?"

Torey stiffened. Bart wasn't referring to decisions about trees. *You're tired of mush when you could have steak. That itch you've got isn't going to go away on its own. I'd like to be the man to make a real woman out of you.* Oh, no, Bart wasn't talking about trees at all.

Her gaze flicked over him, disdainfully, she hoped. "If you came over here to bait me, just pile back into your truck and get going, Scanlon."

"A little discussion about decisions is baiting you?"

He was still smiling, still doing his best to bedevil her. "You don't even know how to have a little discussion." Turning away, Torey walked a few steps along the fence. "Are you still willing to pay for half of the poplars?"

"Within reason."

"What's within reason, Scanlon?"

Bart leaned against a fence post. "What's with this Scanlon bit, honey? Did you forget my first name?"

She glared. "Can we stop with the games for a few minutes?"

"Sure, Lancaster, whatever you say."

Was it possible to hate anyone more than she hated Bart Scanlon? Maybe what seemed so self-destructive, though, was standing here hating him and still seeing him as a handsome, sexy man. The memory of their sham of a date had a hundred different inflections and caused a roller-coaster run of emotions. She had every right to feel insulted at Bart's mockery and every reason to despise him. But who or what should she blame for weak knees in Bart's presence?

Torey braced herself to ignore Bart's insolence. "I talked to Joe Holcombe about some poplars."

"And?"

"I figure I need twenty-two."

"Twenty-two!" Bart pushed away from the post. He laid his hands on his hips. "How much money are we talking about?"

Torey raised her chin. "Fifty dollars apiece." Bart looked off, obviously calculating a total. "If you want to back down from your offer..." she said coolly, perversely hoping he would. There would be a certain amount of satisfaction in watching Bart renege on an offer. She could see that he was giving it some thought.

"Joe's got cheaper ones, doesn't he?" It seemed like a hell of a waste of money to Bart, in the first place, and he didn't mind saving a buck wherever he could, in the second.

"Smaller ones, yes. I don't want small trees."

Bart formed a lazy grin. "Most of us don't always get what we want. Take me, for instance..."

He was back to the date. The man should have been an actor, Torey thought. She'd never known anyone who could put so much into a few, seemingly innocuous words.

"Not on a silver platter," she drawled.

Bart looked inordinately chagrined, a decided exaggeration, Torey felt. "Aw, shucks! And there I was going to ask you out tonight."

He was kidding, wasn't he? He didn't really have the gall to invite her out for another evening of dodging kisses and insults? Something hot and vital leaped through Torey's veins at the thought of Bart's kisses, but her mind was working and she quickly squelched the unwanted reaction.

"I already have a date," she said sweetly, pleased to be in the position of announcing that she certainly didn't need Bart Scanlon to get out of the house at night.

He cocked an eyebrow. "With...don't tell me. I'll get it." He snapped his fingers, as though remembering the name only with great effort. "John Stevenson, right?"

"You know perfectly well his name is Steve Johnson! Damn, you're irritating, Scanlon!"

Bart grinned. "Bet you'd have more fun with me."

"Like last time? That was really a great date, wasn't it?"

"It could have been."

Torey's face was flaming. "If I would have cooperated, you mean? Wrestling on the seat of a pickup is hardly my idea of a fun date!"

"Oh? Where do you prefer to do your...wrestling? Wait a minute. I thought we'd already established the fact that you haven't done much—" Bart cleared his throat "—wrestling. I've got a few holds you might be interested in. Might help you tonight with John."

"*Steve!*" Torey yelled. Breathing fast and furiously, she spun around and started away. "Oh, go bother someone else! Go cut some trees down! Go to hell!"

"Make up your mind," Bart called cheerily. "I'm good, honey, but not good enough to be in three places at the same time."

Torey was just going around the back of the house when she heard Bart yell, "What about the poplars?" She hesitated a moment, then kept on going. To hell with the poplars, too!

Six

The Saturday night date with Steve passed pleasantly enough. Steve never teased or taunted. He listened to her end of normal conversation and agreed with Torey's opinion on most of the topics they touched on. Torey caught herself studying the young veterinarian at various points of the evening. Steve wore his brown hair in a very short, controlled style. He had a pleasant, attractive face, and the man shone with cleanliness. He had a gentle way of speaking and moving, and Torey knew that he was a steady, levelheaded person. All in all, Steve Johnson would make some woman a very good husband.

But when he kissed her good-night, Torey knew it wouldn't be her. As nice as Steve was, she felt nothing special when he touched her. He smelled good, but his scent wasn't the least arousing. Bart Scanlon excited her more in one minute than Steve did in four hours. That Bart's brand of excitement was dangerous and something she knew she should stay away from didn't seem to diminish it. Just thinking about Bart raised her blood pressure.

Torey didn't sleep very well that night, unable to escape the feeling that she was on the brink of doing something foolish. She kept thinking of Bart's insolently stated, "Aw shucks! And there I was going to ask you out tonight."

Was it true, or just another one of Bart's incessant gibes?

If he had actually had the nerve to ask for another date and she hadn't already been busy, what would her answer have been?

The boys she'd dated in high school and the men since flitted through Torey's mind. None of them, even the few she had really liked, had caused the tumult that Bart was causing. Never had she had such raw, unpredictable emotions to deal with. *Nor* such battered pride, she reminded herself. She didn't want to like Bart Scanlon, but liking wasn't the right word for what she felt for him. Lord, how could it be, when there were moments, like this morning by the fence, when she wanted to strangle him? In all honesty, Torey didn't know the right word to describe her feelings for Bart, or even if there was one.

Analyzing it over and over again did no good. When Bart was in her thoughts, physical discomfort was in her body. Heat curled and uncurled within her, like a hand clasping and unclasping. The more she tried to think it through and get Bart out of her mind once and for all, the deeper he became embedded.

By morning, Torey had slept only a few sporadic hours, and at the first sign of dawn, she threw back the covers, weary of struggling with the problem. After splashing water on her face and brushing her teeth, she quietly got dressed, tiptoed to the kitchen and scrawled a note for Lorna. *Took one of the horses for a ride. If I'm not back by nine, go to church without me.*

Without further delay, Torey plucked a banana and an orange from the fruit bowl, settled her old hat on her head and left the house. The early dawn air was almost chilly, and it felt wonderful to her cobwebby brain. Torey ate the banana on the walk to the barn, tossed the peel into a trash barrel, then stood over the receptacle and peeled the orange. Eating the sections, one by one, she eyed the horse pasture and decided which horse to ride.

Nothing docile today. She wanted to feel power beneath her and a strong mouth holding the reins. She wanted to have to consciously maintain control of her mount; maybe a long, tiring ride would drive Bart Scanlon out of her brain.

Fifteen minutes later Torey was riding Nero, a large black stallion with a mouth of iron. She knew her arms would ache tonight, but maybe that ache would displace a few others she was getting tired of battling.

It was disappointingly upsetting to understand so completely that Bart's lewd suggestions that night hadn't obliterated his fascination. She'd been fighting mad for a while—hell, she was still mad. But there was also something very exciting about a man talking so plainly. She could have Bart, if she wanted him. It might be for ten minutes, it might be for longer. Torey had no way of knowing what kind of lover Bart would be, although wishful thinking was beginning to shape a romanticized portrayal of smoldering passion that seemed unrealistic, even to her.

Regardless, silly fantasies or not, the hand clasping and unclasping in her stomach was real enough for anyone. Steve was not going to dispel it, nor was anyone else.

Except Bart.

Groaning under her breath, Torey turned Nero's big head toward the mountains. At least Sundays were free of those annoying growls and piercing buzzes that Bart's logging equipment sent echoing across the valley. She knew the buzzing was from the chain saws used to cut down the trees, but she didn't know what else went on since she'd never seen a real logging operation.

This was a good time to take a look at Bart's project. It wasn't likely that anyone was on the mountain today.

Yes, why not? Torey decided. It had been ages since she'd crossed her own fence line and ridden on Scanlon land, anyway. She'd have to double-back a little, just to reach a stock gate, but that wouldn't take long.

Once she was on Bart's land, Torey turned Nero west. The road Bart was building was a long, ugly slash heading east, falling behind horse and rider as they progressed. Torey spotted stakes then, narrow slats of wood with orange-painted tops, apparently delineating the roadway on to the mountain. Following the stakes should bring her directly to the logging site, she realized.

As Nero climbed, the terrain changed. Treeless grassland gave way to sparse, scattered trees, and then rather quickly changed to a forest. The underbrush became thicker, the trees taller, but the stakes were easy to follow.

It was a pleasant ride. Sunlight filtered through the pine trees and the woods smelled fresh and damp. And then Torey began to see signs of logging, some downed trees, piles of branches and apparently unusuable lengths of pine, some stumps.

Nero burst into a clearing before Torey even knew it was there. She couldn't believe her own eyes for a minute: Bart was up on a big machine with a long crane attachment, and he was looking as surprised as she felt.

"I *thought* I heard something," he said with a laugh, and began scrambling to the ground.

"Don't . . . I mean . . ." Torey was definitely off balance. She'd been so sure no one would be here.

Bart walked over and took hold of Nero's bridle, patting the big horse's nose at the same time. He glanced up at Torey. "Get down," he said softly.

There was a challenge in that soft voice, and it sent a skittering warning prickle up Torey's spine. "No. I didn't mean to interrupt anyone." Torey really didn't know what to do. She had no business being here, and Bart was probably thinking that she'd come looking for him. He was bareheaded and without those concealing dark glasses he'd had on yesterday morning. Of course, he didn't need them here. Everything was shaded and cool, a little sun-speckled, but more shadowed than anything else. Torey ripped her gaze from Bart's deep blue eyes and looked around. There were big yellow pieces of machinery in the clearing.

"Get down and I'll give you the grand tour," Bart suggested. "Ever been around a logging site before?"

Torey cleared her throat. "No, thank you. I was just taking a ride and sort of . . . drifted this way."

Bart laughed right out loud. "You *drifted* across two strands of barbed wire? Come off it, Torey. You deliberately came up here."

Her face warmed. "I didn't know you'd be here."

"Did I say you did?" Bart was strangely pleased about his visitor. He never could have imagined Torey coming up here, but now that she had, he didn't want her to immediately ride away. "Come on, get down and stay awhile."

"I'm not really interested in machinery," Torey confessed, suspecting that Bart's grand tour would be a narrative on his logging equipment.

Bart slid the reins through his hand as he came closer to the black's saddle. "We won't even mention machinery," he promised, reaching Torey's hands on the reins with his own. Letting go then, he encircled her waist. Torey sucked in a startled breath. Bart's big hands around her waist burned clear through her jeans and shirt.

He smiled teasingly. "Come on, cutie. Get down."

Cutie? If she got off of Nero, anything might happen! Panicked, Torey yanked on the reins, intending to turn Nero away from Bart. The big horse reared up on his hind legs and whinnied. "What the hell?" Bart cried, and jumped back. But only for a split second. While Torey tried to calm the stallion, Bart leaped forward and grabbed the bridle again. "Easy, boy," he muttered. "Take it easy."

Torey was tightly grasping the reins. She was a good rider, but Nero had a temper and a mind of his own. It was Bart who was making him nervous, though. "Just stand away from him," Torey demanded.

"What the hell are you doing riding a horse like this?"

"I beg your pardon!" Icicles dripped from the words. "I hardly need your approval on which horse I choose to ride."

"This is a stallion."

"No," Torey drawled scornfully. "You're kidding."

"He's too much for a woman like you to handle."

"He most certainly is not! Let go of the bridle, Scanlon!"

He gave her a look that probably could have curdled milk, Torey saw with a sinking sensation. Another warning bell went off in her system when she saw Bart working his way to the saddle again. "All right, this time I'm not asking," he said with a dark scowl, and reached for her.

Torey was so neatly removed from the saddle, she couldn't believe it. She had automatically loosened her right foot from the stirrup when she felt herself being lifted, simply because she wasn't sure what Bart would do if she got hung up. It seemed much too melodramatic to think he might rip her leg off, but the thought did flash through her mind. There was little she would put past Bart, she realized again.

Then, just as she'd feared, Bart didn't set her feet on the ground. He held her up and to him, leaving her boots dangling several inches off of the dark Montana soil and well-trampled vegetation. Her hat fell off when she tipped her face up to glower into his. "Just what do you think you're doing?"

"Holding you."

"Well, stop holding me!" Bart Scanlon's arms were as solid as granite around her. Torey's arms were free, though, and she placed her hands on his shoulders and pushed.

Bart laughed uproariously. "You haven't got the strength of a gnat."

"Put me down!"

Bart let her slide down his body a little, just until the toes of her boots made contact with the ground. "There, you're down."

"Let go of me, Bart."

"Hey, you do remember my first name!"

They were so close, a piece of paper couldn't have been wedged in between them. Bart's outlaw grin was about level with the top of Torey's head. If she didn't keep her head back, her face would be buried in Bart's soft, blue work shirt. She could smell him, and Bart's odors were completely masculine and uniquely him. His body was as hard as his arms, and yet she felt it yielding to her less rigid flesh. Impossibly, his chest seemed to be molding around her breasts, and his hips cradled hers with an insistent pressure.

His expression slowly changed, his eyes growing darker. "Am I hurting you?"

She could have lied and said yes, but the drumming of her blood provoked honesty. "No," she whispered.

"Why did you come here?"

She hesitated. Insisting that she'd merely "drifted" to his mountain was silly. "Curiosity, I guess." His body stirred, small ripples beneath his clothes that managed to unite them even more intimately.

Bart's voice was low. "You couldn't have known I was here."

"Of course not."

"Curiosity about the logging operation, then?"

Torey nodded once. "We...could talk better if we weren't so..."

His gaze roamed her face. "What's going on with us, Torey?"

"Nothing," she whispered huskily. She knew Bart was feeling the same crazy thrills she was. She could see it on his face, in his eyes. The tanned skin of his throat gave way to the black hair on his chest, and she flicked a glance at the tufts so close to her face. She wet her dry lips, completely aware of Bart's ruthless stare.

He rolled his hips slightly. "Nothing?"

A flush heated Torey's face. He was getting very aroused from this clinch and was arrogant enough to point it out. "How long are we going to stand here?" she demanded, putting reproach in the question.

Bart's eyes narrowed. "I don't know. Maybe until you stop lying."

"Lying!"

"If not to me, then to yourself. You haven't faced it yet, have you?"

"Faced what?" she bravely challenged, angry that he would accuse her of lying to anyone, even herself.

"Your own needs."

"My needs are my business. Bart, this is getting ridiculous. I feel like a fool."

He grinned lazily. "No, you don't. You feel like a woman."

"To you, maybe."

"To me, definitely. No maybe about it."

Torey knew he was going to kiss her. She'd known it from the moment he'd asked her to get down from Nero, as a matter of fact. Her insides were lurching like a canoe on rapids. Bart was wrong about her not having faced her own needs. She wasn't happy about suddenly discovering her own sexuality, but she'd faced it, and she'd also faced the immutable fact that Bart had caused the whole thing. This was the man with the power to turn her inside out, the only man, and it was totally insane, given their history.

Bart's face came down slowly. The grin was absent from his lips, but a suspect light was in his eyes. If he'd only kiss her in a serious vein, Torey thought, then recoiled from the idea. Why would she want something serious from Bart Scanlon?

He stopped short of their mouths touching. "You're not saying no."

Her voice was a husky whisper. "Would it do any good?"

"You want me to kiss you, don't you?"

She closed her eyes briefly. "I don't know what I want from you."

"But you want something. You wouldn't be here if you didn't." Bart caressed her lips with his, a butterfly kiss. "I want something, too."

Her breath caught. The fleeting contact of their mouths had ignited a whole new array of emotions. "I know you do."

His lips brushed hers again. Torey's head moved languorously, her mouth seeking his. "Are you still afraid of me?" he whispered, and nibbled at her lips.

"Yes."

"But you're here, anyway."

Her hands rose to the back of his neck, a dreamy expression entering her eyes. "I didn't know you'd be here."

"But you were hoping." Bart's arms relaxed around her enough to drop lower on her body, and he bent her backwards a little, snugly curving himself around her. His mouth settled down on hers, and moved until he found the perfect fit. Then, with a long sigh of pleasure, the kiss became important.

Torey was light-headed from the sensations of Bart's body wrapped around hers, his scent, the way he kissed. His mouth was perfection, just full enough, just firm enough. His tongue slipped between her lips in an unhurried, mesmerizing movement. A small whimper built in her throat.

Bart raised his head and looked at her. His eyes were smoky with desire. Torey looked back. Neither was breathing very well. "I'm glad you came," he said softly.

"Are you?" she whispered, so shaken she was afraid she would fall if he suddenly let go of her.

Bart looked around, frowning then. "This is a hell of a place for..."

Torey knew exactly what he meant. *This is a hell of a place for making love.* Bart fully intended in taking the next giant step in a relationship that she was still afraid of! She loved his kisses. Bart Scanlon's kisses were like none she'd ever experienced. And she wondered—oh, did she wonder!—about what else he was so expert at. Torey knew what was causing all the stressful aches in her body, and she wasn't afraid of sex, but the idea of getting so deeply involved with Bart scared the stuffing out of her. With one condescending look or a few scathing words Bart could practically destroy her. He'd done it all of their lives. He was being nice right now, but what if, after the fun was over, he reverted back to his usual cynical self?

Torey honestly didn't think she could bear such humiliation. She wished he could be content with kisses and getting to know each other better!

She tried to extricate herself from Bart's hold and he raised an eyebrow in a quizzical look. "Backing down again?"

She could have gotten instantly angry, Torey realized. But she was beginning to catch glimpses of something that warranted a little patience. "I'd like to just talk," she said quietly.

"Talk?" Laughing humorlessly, Bart looked away. Talking wasn't what he wanted to do, although he remembered acknowledging that he and Torey had never just talked. Right this minute, though, the throb in his loins made talking pretty unattractive. Still, as he'd commented, this wasn't much of a place for lovemaking. Again, he got the sense of wanting the best for Torey Lancaster. She deserved satin sheets and soft pillows beneath her while he made slow, delicious love to her, not a quicky encounter in the rough surroundings of smelly machinery and piles of dead brush.

Bart brought his gaze back to the lush woman in his arms. He wasn't above doing a little bargaining. "If I talk now, will you see me this afternoon?"

Torey tried to steady the renewed rush of her pulse. "Are you asking for a trade-off?"

"I'm asking you to see me this afternoon."

"To do what?" she weakly inquired, almost afraid of the answer.

"Whatever comes naturally, honey."

The cynical note back in Bart's drawl alerted Torey. For a few minutes there he'd spoken like anyone else. A very strange thought flashed through Torey's mind: Beneath the cynical, sardonic man Bart showed the world—or, at least, her—was a perfectly normal human being! Why did he work so diligently to keep her from knowing that man?

The whole thing astounded Torey, but it also excited her. She seemed to be irreversibly drawn to Bart, and if there was more to him than chemistry and wisecracks, she wanted to know what it was.

"All right, fine," she said evenly. "I'll see you this afternoon."

Every time Torey agreed with anything he said or suggested, Bart was surprised. Probably because she never had until recently. But because he always had trouble believing the change in her, he couldn't resist teasing just a little. "Another kiss, then I'll let you go."

She'd lost her objections to kissing Bart, and teasing *him* wasn't totally out of the question, either. Torey smiled seductively, playing with fire and knowing it. There was something exceedingly heady about knowing this sexy, fascinating man really did want her, and she dampened and parted her lips in invitation.

"Careful," he growled in a playful warning as he brought his lips down on hers. In seconds the playfulness was gone. He was breathing hard and wanting more than a ripe, tempting mouth under his. A vision of undressing Torey Lancaster, of having her naked and writhing beneath him, was so vivid in his mind, he was starting to change his opinion of this being an impossible place in which to make love. There were ways, there were *always* ways if desire was strong enough.

Her hands were in his hair, her fingers twisting and threading through it. Bart raggedly whispered against her lips. "Doing what comes naturally is going to knock us both out, honey." And then he raised his head and frowned. "Here comes Rob and Rich. Great timing, huh?"

The sound of a vehicle was getting more noticeable. Torey was staring at Bart's mouth through passion-glazed eyes. How many times would he have to kiss her before she forgot everything else and did anything he wanted? "Were you expecting them?" she whispered thickly.

Bart studied her flushed face. "You're so beautiful you take my breath away." He moved against her, slowly, suggestively, then shook his head and backed away, releasing Torey so abruptly she teetered. "Yeah, I was expecting them. And if I don't cool down, they're both going to know what we've been doing." He grinned. "Or, almost doing."

Dazed, Torey watched him walk into the woods and disappear. She looked for Nero then and spotted the big horse grazing a short distance away. A pickup sped into the clearing, stirring up dust. Its windows were down and a blast of deafening music continued after the motor was turned off. The Scanlon twins jumped out, stared at Torey, then glanced at each other.

"Hi," she called.

"Hello, Torey," they said in unison, walking over to her. One of them—Torey never could tell them apart—asked, "Where's Bart?"

"He's around," she said weakly. "I didn't know you guys worked on Sunday, too." Rob and Rich Scanlon were very handsome young men, reminding her of Bart in high school. They had Bart's coloring and lanky build, and even that same devilish light in their eyes.

"We always lube and service the equipment on Sunday," one young Scanlon said.

"Oh, I see." *Where was Bart?* "Well, I was just taking a ride on Nero there, and..." With relief, Torey saw Bart returning.

He greeted his brothers with a grin and, "Turn the radio down, boys. At this volume, the citizens of Stanton are probably covering their ears."

Torey started for Nero. "I'll be running along. Nice seeing you all."

Bart followed her, and when Torey had swung up into the saddle, he said softly, "About three?"

She hesitated, then nodded. "All right, three."

"See you then." Bart stepped back.

When she was gone, he ambled back to his brothers. "I don't believe it," Rob drawled. "Torey Lancaster?"

"Anything wrong with Torey Lancaster?" Bart said quietly.

"Not if you're looking for the marrying kind, there isn't," the young man quipped.

Bart laughed. "The voice of experience, right?" But while he got to work on the equipment, it occurred to him that Rob was right. Torey *was* the kind of woman men married. What the hell was he getting himself into?

Seven

After church on Sunday morning, Torey and Lorna would often stop at one restaurant or another for brunch. Assuming Lorna had found someone else to share the meal with, Torey wasn't at all alarmed that the house was empty when she returned at noon.

She fixed herself some scrambled eggs and toast, straightened the kitchen, then went to take a shower. The telephone rang before she got completely undressed. It was Lorna. "Torey? I'm over at the Kendricks place. Myra insisted I come home and spend the day with her and Paul."

"Oh, that's fine, Lorna. I'm going out, anyway."

"Great. Well, don't look for me until after dinner tonight. Probably around seven. Myra's planning a big meal. I just wanted you to know where I am."

"Thanks, Lorna. Have a good time."

Lorna had hordes of friends scattered around the countryside, and she often spent Sunday afternoons away from the ranch. It struck Torey, however, while she finished undressing and stepped into the shower, that she would be alone when Bart came to pick her up.

Thinking of Bart created a symphony of emotions, a return and then some of everything she'd felt on the mountain. Torey was more positive than ever that Bart wasn't what she'd always thought. Oh, there was no doubting the irritating traits he seemed to have honed to a fine art. But there was something else beneath all of that derision and mockery. She'd caught only a glimpse of it today, yet it had aroused a desire to investigate further.

Was it possible that Bart's pessimistic exterior concealed a gentle man? One who was maybe a tad vulnerable and preferred no one understanding that? Torey recalled the remark Bart had made on that first date about being romantic with the right woman. It had struck her as peculiarly uncharacteristic that night, and it still did. Bart was hiding something, maybe only subconsciously, but there were layers to his personality that Torey knew she hadn't gotten near.

Along with that intriguing aspect, the man was undeniably magnetic, a dynamite combination. For the first time in her twenty-eight years, she was completely immersed in the perplexities of what made a particular man tick. She'd mentioned talking today, and Bart had agreed. She knew it was only because of where they were, and even at that, they hadn't gotten to it. But they might have, if the twins hadn't come along.

That's where she should set her sights this afternoon, on simple conversation. She already knew that he didn't take time for music, and apparently did for hunting, but what about other things? Did he enjoy sports? Reading? What were his political views? Not that she wanted to get into an involved political discussion, but it would be nice to know just a few facts about Bart's personal preferences. She certainly had no qualms about admitting hers.

Torey was drying off when she stopped dead in her tracks. Talk about getting the cart before the horse! One tiny peek into Bart Scanlon's psyche, and she was thinking of him as a regular guy! Was she forgetting his ability to crush her? To infuriate her? To *destroy* her? Look what he'd done out at the fence yesterday with very simple tools, Steve's name and twenty-two poplar trees!

Torey's heart sank. Fooling around with Bart was still very dangerous business. Forgetting that would be extremely shortsighted.

Frowning, not quite so thrilled with the upcoming date, Torey proceeded with her drying off at a slower pace. Thinking more clearly, she admitted that only a complete fool wouldn't know what Bart wanted from Torey Lancaster. He'd never once tried to conceal it or gloss it over with pretty phrases. Should she conclude that if he got what he seemed to want so badly, that would be the end of it?

Deflated and slightly disgusted with her earlier meanderings, Torey slipped into a light robe and laid on her bed. How easily he led her, she thought reflectively, staring up at the ceiling. He could make her crazy with innuendo or completely senseless with kisses, but whichever direction he took off in, she followed along as if she didn't have a mind of her own.

Why did she do that with Bart when she never had with any other man? Did he have a stronger personality than anyone else she'd ever encountered?

Yawning, Torey glanced at the clock on the bedstand. She had time for a nap, and after little sleep last night and the long ride on Nero, she was ready for one. Turning to her side, she got comfortable and closed her eyes. She may as well nap if she could; if she didn't, all she would do was torture herself trying to figure out Bart Scanlon.

* * *

After greasing and servicing the equipment at the logging site, Bart and the twins returned to their house. "One hour of cleaning, then you guys can go off with your friends," Bart announced firmly.

Rob and Rich groused, but they certainly couldn't argue that the house didn't need cleaning. Not when it was getting tough to even plow through it. All three of them changed to old cutoff jeans and dug in.

Bart took the kitchen, Rich started the laundry and worked on the bathrooms and Rob tackled the living room. In an hour, the house was far from being really clean, but the improvement was incredible. The twins quickly showered, dressed and took off, and Bart shook his head and laughed as they disappeared. He didn't like making the boys work on Sunday, not when they put in a full week at the logging site. But summers were short, and the Scanlons were committed to making hay while the sun shone, so to speak.

Seeing that he had an hour before picking up Torey, Bart took a leisurely shower, then did another load of laundry. At ten minutes to three, wearing clean jeans, a white shirt and his best boots, he left the house, patted the three dogs who were always looking for a kind word, got in his pickup and headed for the highway. He liked it when chores and jobs were done and behind him, and he whistled between his teeth as he drove.

Right at the highway, though, he spotted something else that needed doing, the replacement of some rotten posts in his fence. The ranch ran a sizable herd of cattle, and it was easy to get caught up in the logging operation and put off ranch chores.

Enough time to keep everything going was a problem, and here he was going off to spend the rest of the day with Torey Lancaster. And Torey was the marrying kind of woman, too. Just what was her big draw? Why couldn't he turn this pickup around and drop in on one of the several attractive women he knew who weren't looking for matrimony?

Well, maybe there was no such thing. But some of his female friends didn't act like marriage was all that important.

As for him, he had the twins to get through college and medical school. Maybe then...

Bart stopped the pickup beside the Lancaster house. The car was gone, but Torey's pickup was parked in a two-vehicle garage with the doors up. The place seemed extraordinarily quiet.

He went to the back door and knocked. After a minute, he knocked again. Glancing back at the garage, Bart wondered if Torey had stood him up. Maybe she and Lorna had taken the car and gone off somewhere.

The door opened. Torey stood there, squeezing her robe together at her throat. Her hair was mussed and tousled, her face completely devoid of cosmetics. "Oh, Bart, I'm sorry. I only meant to sleep a few minutes."

She looked warm and youthful and utterly beautiful, and Bart felt a strange contraction in his midsection. "Did Nero wear you out?"

Torey was apprehensive. If Lorna was home, or yes, if Steve was her date, she wouldn't worry about getting ready with a man in the house. But Bart wasn't Steve Johnson, nor even remotely like Steve. Torey knew if she left Steve in the living room, she could parade naked through the rest of the house and he'd never know it. Bart, on the other hand, might prowl around and do anything. Once he realized they were alone in the house, there was no telling *what* he might do.

"Nero was part of it, but I didn't sleep very well last night."

"Didn't your date with—" Bart grinned wickedly, and Torey fully expected him to stumble over Steve's name again. As usual, Bart did just the opposite "—Steve go well?"

She wasn't going to discuss Steve, certainly not with Bart. "It was nothing like that," she said firmly, which it hadn't been. Bart had kept her awake, not Steve.

"Aren't you going to invite me in?"

Troubled, Torey wasn't able to keep her quandary off her face. "Well... Lorna's not here," she confessed reluctantly, and knew immediately, from the devilish glint in Bart's eyes, that she'd been right to doubt the wisdom of inviting him in when she was alone. "Would you mind waiting on the patio?"

"Yeah, I would," he replied casually.

"You would?"

Laughing, Bart reached out and flicked the sash of her robe. "Invite me in, Torey," he drawled softly.

Beneath the flimsy cotton robe, Torey's nudity mocked her. Why hadn't she set the alarm on the clock? she wondered frantically. There was absolutely no reason for her to be in this embarrassing situation, and it was certainly setting the wrong tone for the kind of date she'd hoped this one would be. How would she ever get Bart to just talk when she'd started his motor running by answering the door in a bathrobe? Anyone with half a brain and even poor eyesight would be able to tell that she had very little on under the pale pink robe. Bart was neither stupid nor blind, and she'd always suspected him of having X-ray vision, anyway.

Bart rubbed the side of his face. "What am I gonna do with you, Torey?"

"What are *you* going to do with *me?*"

"Yes. You advance and retreat faster than greased lightning. I don't know how to read you. Does Steve what's-his-face understand you?"

"Please don't start that again."

"All right, Steve Johnson. Does he go along with your games?"

"My games! In the first place, *like* I already told you, Steve and I are only friends. In the second, I don't consider a certain amount of reserve as playing games."

Bart shook his head disgustedly. "So, we're back to fighting, huh? Well, I think I'm getting just a little tired of this whole scene." Hell, he might as well go back home and finish the laundry, he was thinking.

Torey's mouth dropped as Bart started away. He was leaving! She didn't want him to leave! "Bart!"

He stopped and looked back at her. "Yeah?"

With a burning face and sweaty palms, Torey swallowed her pride. "Please. Just give me five minutes."

Bart couldn't believe this. His simplistic analysis of Torey Lancaster suddenly developing a libido wasn't the whole story here, not when he'd made it so plain a dozen times that he was at her disposal and she kept avoiding what he'd really thought she wanted.

Unless she was such a damned prude she kept fighting herself.

Speculatively, Bart walked back to the stoop. "And then?"

Torey cleared her throat. "And then we'll talk."

Deliberately Bart glanced at the patio with its four chairs, two lounges and one glass-topped table. "Out here, right?"

"Not necessarily. I thought we had a date. Where were you going to take me?"

"I thought we might drive to Billings for supper."

"Well, what's wrong with that?"

Putting his hands on his hips, Bart walked a small circle. Maybe it was time to get something across to Torey Lancaster. If all she saw in the present arrangement was a reason to keep him out on the patio, she had some pretty screwy ideas about where their relationship might be going. Deliberately, he hit her with a hard look. "I'm not looking for a wife, Torey."

Her skin paled, then turned crimson. "And you think that I'm looking for a husband? You insufferable clod! If I was, which I'm not, I certainly wouldn't be looking at you!" Jerking backwards, Torey grabbed the edge of the door, fully intending to slam it off its hinges. Through a haze of furious red, however, she saw Bart also grab the door, and he easily stopped her from closing it.

He came in, and Torey backed up some more. Her eyes had narrowed to slits. "Get out of my house," she said through clenched teeth.

Bart closed the door and leaned against it. "I will. But before I do, I'm going to say something."

"Oh, not another one of your inspiring speeches, I hope!"

"Call it what you want. You and I have one thing in common, Torey, that fence out there. Until you grow up, let's keep it at that, all right? Don't come pussyfooting into my logging camp, or parading yourself all over the place every time I inspect my new road. Oh, I've seen you, don't think I haven't."

"You're insane! I haven't paraded myself, and I don't give one hoot and holler how many times you look at your stupid road."

Bart began to turn around to the door, then he hesitated. "If you were half the woman you think you are, you would have seen the opportunity we had today. Neither one of us is alone very much. You've got Lorna and I've got the twins."

"Maybe I saw it and didn't want it. Maybe I don't want *you!* Hasn't that occurred to you, Scanlon, or are you too conceited to face the possibility that not every woman in Montana is panting after you?"

Bart's eyes narrowed. "Oh, you're panting, all right. But you don't have any guts, *Lancaster*. There's nothing you want more than a real man. For some ungodly reason, you suddenly realized you had one living on the next ranch, but you'll never do anything about it."

Torey made a tactical error then. She lunged at Bart, willing to risk anything if she could just wipe that smug, superior expression off his face. When she raised her hand, her robe swirled and parted below the sash at her waist, exposing bare skin from toenails to mid-thighs. Bart looked, but only briefly, too busy intercepting a slap on the face to linger on the pretty sight.

Holding her wrist in a relentless grip, he yanked her forward. His eyes were dark and angry. "Do you know what the height of folly is, sweetheart? Well, let me give you a hint. I don't believe in men slapping women around, but a woman your size trying to slap me isn't exactly smart, either, now is it?"

Torey swallowed hard. She was burning with humiliation. She had never, ever attempted to slap someone before, and Bart was right. If she would have struck him and he had slapped her back, she might be on the floor right now. "I'm sorry," she whispered. "I'm terribly sorry. There's never been another person who could make me as angry as you do."

"I affect you in a lot of ways."

"Yes," she said in a low, tense voice.

"I always did."

"Not...the way you do now."

Remembering the swirling pink cotton around her long, tanned legs, Bart sucked in a quick breath. Torey affected

him, too. She always had. The top of the robe was gaping,
allowing a glimpse of a smooth breast. He couldn't see the
nipple, but the sweet slope of female flesh was getting to
him. "But you keep fighting it," he said, noting the ragged edge his voice was taking on.

"I don't want to be another notch on your bedpost."

"My reputation precedes me, apparently. Torey, most of
it is just stupid gossip."

"You're hurting my wrist."

Bart relaxed his hand, but he didn't let go. Instead, gazing into her eyes, he gently wound her arm around her
back, bringing her breasts in contact with his chest. "Put
your other arm around my neck. Kiss me the way you want
to," he urged hoarsely. His free hand found the knot of the
sash at her waist and began to undo it.

All the fight had deserted Torey. She'd shocked herself
by her fury, and she was really so weary of holding Bart off
when what she wanted was to have him kiss her until she
didn't care what he did. He knew it, too, she saw in the co-
balt-blue depths of his eyes. He knew he'd won.

It didn't matter. While he untied the knot in the sash, she
slid her hand up his chest, slowly, savoring the territory she
journeyed over to reach the back of his neck. She saw him
react to her fingers moving in the hair covering that sensitive area, and then react again when he parted the robe and
looked down at her. Today, on the mountain, he'd said she
was so beautiful she took his breath away. Now, she saw it
happening.

"Torey..." His mouth covered hers in a kiss of complete possession. He released his hold on the wrist he'd
taken behind her back to free both of his hands, and they
slid into the robe's opening, sliding again as he began exploring, this time over her skin. He held her breasts, then
followed the inward curve of her waist. He traced the female shape of her hips, then did it all again.

"You're incredible," he whispered, raising her temperature another notch by the intensity in his rusty-sounding voice. "I want you. You want me, too. Say it, tell me you do." Bart's right hand caressed a hot trail down her abdomen. Her eyes opened, giving him access to her inner thoughts. "Can you tell me?" He moved his hand lower, through the silky hair at the meeting of her thighs, and then deeper into the secrets of her body.

Torey's lips parted. Her eyelids drooped a little. "I want you," she whispered. "You know I do."

He curved an arm around the back of her neck, resting her head in the crook of his elbow, and kissed her lips. His right hand stayed where it had been, gently stroking, giving her both pleasure and torment. The kiss became more needful as Torey's breathing increased. Her mind was spinning. Bart's expertise was sinfully delicious. His tongue moved in and out of her mouth, and she felt assaulted with delirious sensations.

The heat and thrills compounded until she was moaning deep in her throat. "Take me to your room." It was an urgent whisper against her lips. Torey's eyes fluttered open again. Bart's were hooded, dark, penetrating, and looking into them, she knew she was lost.

"Down that hall."

His mouth moved, just a little, forming only the hint of a smile. Then he bent slightly, put one arm behind her thighs and swept her up off of the floor. "The second door," Torey whispered, clinging to his neck and burying her face in his shirt. She was on fire, with every nerve ending causing distress.

Bart put her down gently on her own bed, then stood up, pulled his shirt out of his jeans, and began unbuttoning it. His gaze moved over her. The robe was open, only connected to Torey at all by its sleeves. She didn't attempt to close it. Bart's intensely admiring inspection was annihilating inhibitions, vanquishing doubts. The impact of hot blue eyes was like a burn on her skin. Her nipples were puckered and upright, aching for his touch.

She watched him undress, hypnotized by the masculine beauty unfolding before her. Bart's naked shoulders and upper arms were thickly muscled. The black hair she'd seen at the neck of his shirts was a dense, triangular patch, then a narrow line down his tight belly. He took off his boots and socks, then reached for the brass buckle on his belt. Torey stared, unable to turn her eyes away.

Her curiosity was exciting to Bart. She made a beautiful picture lying there, waiting for him. He wanted to sink into her, to lose himself in her soft, female flesh. It would be very easy to forget everything but his own pleasure. He was inordinately worked up, wanting and needing a woman's heat and moisture more than he could ever remember.

Yet, this moment and this woman were somehow very special. There'd been times in the distant past when he would have given almost anything to be where he was now, in Torey Lancaster's bedroom with her all but naked on the bed and wanting him. Then, there'd been years when he hadn't let himself think of Torey. She'd come back into his life because of that road, and there was something ironic about a point of purely cussed dissension causing this.

Bart didn't turn away. He unzipped his fly and pushed his jeans and undershorts down, stepping out of them and leaving them in a heap on the floor. He'd seen Torey's sudden intake of air when the jeans went, but that reaction only fueled his ardor. Everything Torey did increased his desire. In truth, if she did nothing more than lie there and look sensuously beautiful, he would want her more than he'd ever wanted any other woman.

But she didn't just lie there. While he moved to the bed, she slipped the sleeves of the robe off, and the arms she held up to him were bare and silky soft. Like the rest of her.

Bart stretched out on the bed, lying on his side, propped up by an elbow. The smoldering light in his eyes deepened, flickered, as he put a hand on her hip and caressed it. His gaze traveled upward from there, taking in the taut skin of her stomach, and then the full, arousing swells of her breasts. Her nipples were dark rose and pouty. His eyes jumped from them to Torey's face, and stared directly into hers. "Say something," he whispered.

"What would you like me to say?" He was so utterly beautiful, every inch of him, that Torey was still thinking of that moment when she'd finally seen all of him. His legs were not dark like his skin was from the waist up, something she remembered having wondered about. They were long and well-shaped and hairy, but paler than his chest and arms and face.

He bent his head and pressed a tender kiss to her shoulder. "Whatever you're thinking."

Torey blushed, and Bart laughed softly. "That wild, huh? Me, too." He took her hand then and brought it to his chest. "Touch me."

Her eyes were huge gray pools. It wasn't that she'd needed an invitation to touch him—she was more than ready to explore—but she was still a little hesitant with Bart, not quite sure that this gentle, tender side of him would last.

"Touch me everywhere," he whispered when her fingers curled into the hair on his chest. Her pulse leaped, but she slid her hand down his belly. His face neared hers, and then he was pressing her head into the pillow with a heavy, overwhelming kiss. His mouth had opened over hers, and his tongue wet her lips before slipping in between them.

He was very big, and when he threw a thigh over hers, Torey felt completely surrounded by sexually-aroused brawn. The hard length of his manhood pressed into her hip, and it was obvious he was getting a great deal of pleasure out of moving it against her. The sensuous rhythm gave her pleasure, too. Within the staggering desire his body and mouth were creating, she felt his hand moving on her breasts, chafing one nipple, then the other.

And then, quite suddenly, all of the heat and unsettling, disturbing desire she'd been feeling for weeks came together. She tore her mouth from his to cry out as the fist in her body relented into waves of utter bliss. "Bart," she whimpered, pressing her tear-dampened face into his shoulder.

"You're wonderful," he whispered, extremely pleased that she was so responsive. His hands moved over her, caressing her from breasts to thighs, again and again.

Torey was aware of his hands, but she was still trembling from the force of her climax. Never had she experienced such explosive pleasure. The spasms, weaker now, were still shaking her. This man, Bart Scanlon, had given her something she had only touched on in the past. Had she subconsciously known of his power? Felt it and responded to it, despite antagonism and outright hostility?

My Lord, what did she really feel for this outrageous man? Surely a woman didn't let go like this for only a release of sexual tension! Besides, she hadn't had any sexual tension until recently.

Or, had she?

They were both getting sweaty. Bart's hands were sliding on a delicate film of perspiration, and Torey could well feel the dampness on his back beneath her own hands. His lips traveled over her face, then into the soft curve of her throat. He nibbled a few moments, left that fragile spot to capture a rosy nipple, and he began to suck, very gently, very seductively.

A bolt of lightning shot through Torey. Her ability to breathe seemed in sudden jeopardy. Echoes of the last few minutes still ricocheted within her, and she could hardly believe she was responding with even more desire than she'd felt before.

There was no longer a sense of holding back because this was Bart in her bed. Flushed, sweaty, breathing in rushes and gasps, her hands moved over taut muscles and hot skin, gaining through tactile exploration some understanding of the passion contained in Bart's body. It *was* contained, Torey realized, seeing that he'd been holding himself back to give her the utmost pleasure.

Was that what he did with all of his women? The reason for his notable success rate?

Torey squeezed her eyes closed, shying away from the startlingly painful conjecture. She really didn't want to think about anything, and certainly not about Bart and other women.

She'd become as bold as her lover, Torey realized when her hand encountered Bart's most manly part. She felt a shudder in his body when she encircled it. His mouth left her breast and he looked into her eyes. "Are you on the pill?"

Torey's eyes became very large. "No."

Bart moved away from her. "I have something." He reached down to the floor, to his jeans, Torey supposed, and came back up with a small foil-wrapped packet. Her eyes darted away, then returned to watch him sheath himself in fine, soft rubber. It was a moment of complete and utter intimacy, and reached Torey in a whole different way than anything else they'd shared. When he looked at her, he smiled, and she smiled back. For the moment, they were as close as two people could be, she realized.

The interruption had cooled them down a little, but the minute they kissed and touched again, all the hot feelings came rushing back. Torey invited the final step in the most beautiful lovemaking she'd ever been a part of by opening her thighs and whispering, "Make love to me, Bart Scanlon."

His reply was instantaneous. "Gladly, Torey Lancaster."

His gaze held hers while he moved into the V of her legs. "We'll do it this way this first time," he said, surprising Torey. She didn't have the time to analyze Bart's meaning, though, because his body joining hers was much too dominating a theme to think of anything else. When he was deep inside her, he rested on his elbows and looked down at her. "You're perfect," he said in a husky whisper.

She was. The feel of Torey's body around him was thrilling him more than was good for his control. "I want it good for you," he said softly.

She searched the depths of his dark blue eyes. "You've made it good."

"I want it perfect for you." Bart began to move, slowly, clenching his teeth to stop himself from just letting himself go.

Torey touched his mouth. Maybe she shouldn't pursue this, she thought, but Bart's abnormal consideration was actually impossible to accept without question. "Why, Bart?"

Why? Good question. *Damned* good question. Torey was becoming more than a skin-deep itch, and he was starting to tread in dangerous waters. To avoid answering, he kissed her.

She sighed and kissed him back, trailing her fingernails over his shoulders. With each deep thrust of his body, she emitted a small sound, a cross between a moan and a purr. Torey stopped thinking altogether and just let nature take its course. Making love with Bart was incredibly sensual, emotionally energizing. Each movement, each kiss, each caress, created a need for more.

He whispered vividly graphic words in her ear, things that might have shocked her under different circumstances. In his arms, lying beneath him, making love with him, the words heightened her pleasure, seemed to further unite them, in thought as well as body.

She felt him watching her and looked into the blue flame of his eyes. "You're a sensuous woman," he huskily observed.

Her lips parted to catch a breath. "It seems . . . so."

The rhythm gradually increased, in speed, in intensity. Still he watched her. It was almost a mystical experience to be on top of Torey Lancaster and see the passion rising on her beautiful face. A fine veil of perspiration had dampened her temples, making her skin look luminous.

Bart's eyes darkened. He couldn't hold back much longer. What he'd told her was true: He wanted it perfect for her. Dipping his head, he covered her mouth with his, and his tongue took up the same rhythm as their bodies. He reached between them to the small button of sensitive nerve endings within the heat and moisture of her body. In seconds her sounds were only moans; the purring would resume later, he knew.

The moans turned to small cries, then sobs. Torey heard herself as though some amazed part of her was at a great distance, but she'd never felt anything like the rapturous spasms that seemed to be never ending.

She was aware of wildness, of Bart's very active and very vocal completion. She was aware that he called her name at the peak of the turmoil, and then she was aware of his weight, and of how hard he was breathing.

She was so physically replete, she wanted to close her eyes and go to sleep, and then wake up and marvel at what had just happened on her bed.

She knew one thing with complete certainty: She had been very thoroughly made love to. Bart Scanlon, her childhood nemesis, had reached and satisfied the real woman within her.

Eight

With an arm crooked beneath her head, Torey stared into space and waited for Bart to return from the bathroom. She'd drawn her robe up over her for cover, although she wondered if she shouldn't be getting off the bed and putting on some clothes. What time was it?

Turning her eyes to the clock, Torey saw that it was almost five. If Lorna adhered to her usual Sunday afternoon pattern, she would show up around seven.

There was a deeply satisfied jubilation within Torey, a marvelous fulfillment, almost a proud sense of accomplishment. Bart was an incredible lover, strong, caring, giving. During lovemaking, they had communicated so purely, so completely, that Torey felt it had to go deeper than a casual encounter.

She stirred with a moment of uneasiness. Maybe it was more than casual only to her. Maybe caring and giving were

Bart's bedroom techniques and what accounted for his gossiped-about success rate with women.

Placing her fingertips on her temples, Torey rubbed at the tension she was beginning to feel. A sated and satisfied body didn't stop one's thoughts, she realized. A question formed behind her frown: Was she sorry she had finally succumbed to Bart's "dark magnetism"?

It seemed so strange to know Bart as she did now. Not that she understood the machinations of his mind all that well. But to know him on such a physically intimate level was a heady switch in their years-long association. It was really her doing, Torey knew. If she hadn't suddenly seen Bart as a sexy, desirable man, nothing between them would have changed.

As it was, it would no doubt be best for both of them if she could look at today as only an unavoidable collision, a one-time occurrence.

The subject of Torey's speculation strolled into the room with a towel around his middle. "Hope you don't mind. I used your shower."

Some droplets of water glistened on his shoulders and in his hair. Torey's heart fluttered in response to Bart's handsome face and long, lithe frame. "I don't mind," she said quietly. Using her shower wouldn't be a problem in any case, but would she mind anything he decided to do right now? Maybe attempting to view this afternoon as a one-time occurrence was a bit naive.

Her eyes followed his movements. Completely at ease, he dropped the towel and pulled on his underwear, a pair of white briefs. Then he sat on the edge of the bed and looked at her. "Are you okay?"

He had one eyebrow slightly raised, as if half-expecting a negative reply. Maybe the "afterwards" in a "casual" encounter was always somewhat stilted. Torey didn't know, because her few sexual experiences had been with men who'd been important to her, and she to them, even if the relationships hadn't really gone anywhere.

"I'm okay," she said with as much calmness as she could muster.

Bart smiled. "Good." He leaned over and kissed her lips. His mouth was warm and the kiss was sweetly undemanding. Bart's eyes were a little troubled when he raised his head. "A man could get addicted to you very easily, Torey."

"Even against his better judgment?"

He studied her. "Meaning?"

Torey heard just the faintest note of belligerence in the one-word question. The guard he'd dropped during lovemaking was returning, she noted sadly. She didn't want to start trading insults with Bart, not now, not after what they'd shared. She would keep her private thoughts private and hope for the best. That's really all she could do. "Meaning," she said carefully, "that we both knew what we were doing. I'm not asking for anything from you, Bart. You never have to cross that fence out there between our ranches again, if you don't want to."

"And if I do want to?"

Torey took a breath, realizing suddenly that their future relationship was far from decided, but that Bart didn't seem inclined to stop it at this point. It made her head spin, because the prospect had so many avenues of possibility. He didn't want a wife, he'd made that plain. So, an affair? But what kind of affair? Something that would unite them almost as surely as wedding vows, or furtive meetings to have sex when no one was looking? Either scenario had painful aspects, but did she have the strength of will to renounce them?

"Maybe we both have to give it some thought," she said softly and saw a strange relief in his eyes. He was still

studying her, his gaze moving from feature to feature.
"Why are you looking at me so hard?"

"Just enjoying the view, I guess. You're pretty, Torey.
Not only are you a beautiful woman, you're a pretty
woman."

She smiled doubtfully. "Is there a difference?"

"A lot of difference. A woman can be beautiful to look
at without being pretty. Pretty, to me, means feminine,
pleasing. Like the Scots say, bonny." Grinning, he touched
the tip of her nose. "You've got a cute nose, a bonny
nose."

He sobered then. "And a man could get lost in your
eyes."

Torey swallowed the suspect lump that had appeared in
her throat. "You *can* say nice things, can't you? Thank
you."

He hesitated, then laughed. "Yes, I guess I can. I've
given you a bad time in the past, haven't I?"

"Very." Sighing, hating to break this up, Torey glanced
at the clock. "I better get up and get dressed. I don't expect
Lorna until seven, but it would be embarrassing if she
should surprise us by coming home sooner."

"All right," Bart agreed. But instead of moving away, he
brought his head down and kissed her. The kiss was mel-
low, lazily administered, and, Torey felt, designed to initi-
ate a reminder of the afternoon. As though Bart were
saying, "Just so you don't forget what went on here today."

He needn't have worried. If fate should decree that she
never saw Bart Scanlon again, she would still never forget
this day. Indeed, Bart had gotten his wish, the one he'd
stated so crudely on their less than memorable first date: He
had been the man to make a real woman out of her. Or, at
least, a woman who had finally fulfilled the potential of her
own body.

While Bart began dressing, Torey wrapped the robe around herself and went to the closet. Quickly choosing a pair of slacks and a top, she opened a drawer of her dresser for fresh underthings. Then, with her arms full, she hurried away to the bathroom.

On his way through the Lancaster house, Bart stopped at the refrigerator for something to drink. He chuckled at the impressive array of food it contained. His refrigerator was full, too, but not with a plate of fried chicken, a bowl of potato salad and another bowl of what appeared to be home-baked beans. Rob and Rich would wolf this kind of food down like a pack of starving dogs. The twins were bottomless pits; it seemed impossible to ever completely fill them up. He'd been the same at their age.

Reaching for a can of cola, Bart gave a little sigh. His youth seemed like an awfully long time ago, although he was only twelve years away from eighteen, the age of the twins. The past ten years had been tough, though, what with running the ranch and taking care of Rob and Rich. And then when he'd realized their career ambition, he'd geared up even more, determined that they should succeed where he'd failed.

Bart could hear the shower running, and an image of Torey standing under the spray, naked, lushly beautiful, leaped into his mind. He knew there was more to this thing with Torey than he wanted to admit. Frowning then, Bart popped the top on the cola can, went out the back door and settled into a patio chair.

The Lancaster place was a pleasant sight. Colby Lancaster, Torey's grandfather, had been a persnickety old guy, a good rancher, but one who'd gone a step further with his place than most folks around the area. If there'd been one blade of grass off-center when Colby had been alive, Bart would have been surprised. The man's buildings had always been painted before they'd needed it, and from the excellent condition of the place, Bart judged that Torey was following in Colby's footsteps. It was obvious that compared to the Lancaster ranch, the Scanlon place was an eyesore.

The term nudged Bart's memory, and he glanced across the fence to the road under construction. In all honesty, he didn't find the dark streak of overturned earth and waiting equipment at all offensive. But considering Lancaster standards, maybe Torey had a reason to complain. Five-hundred-and-fifty dollars was a lot of money, but he'd told her he would pay for half of the cost of poplars, and he'd stick to his word.

Bart thought of the last two hours. Making love with Torey had been a moving experience. He'd always suspected it would be. Even his adolescent desire to stick his finger in Torey Lancaster's long, auburn curls on the schoolbus had been part of the long-time yen he'd had for her. But where did he want it to go from here?

Bart searched his emotions and knew very well that he wasn't going to go on his merry way and pretend that today hadn't been important. Maybe what was really bothering him was that opinion he'd formed of Torey being the marrying kind of woman. It wasn't that he was against marriage; it was just that he was too committed to ten years of education for his brothers to even *consider* marriage.

So, where did that leave him and Torey?

When Torey came out of the bathroom, it was with the intention of straightening the bed. She stopped at the doorway of her room; the bed had *already* been straightened. It was as neat and wrinkle-free as it had been before she and Bart had made a shambles of it.

Where *was* Bart?

Hurrying through the house, Torey was afraid to think he might have left. Leaving without a word would be a slap in the face she might never get over. She felt almost giddy with relief when she saw him sitting on the patio and took a moment to compose herself before opening the door.

He turned and met her gaze. "Hi."

"Hi. Thanks for making the bed." Torey started for the chair on the other side of him, but when she passed in front of Bart he reached out and pulled her down on his lap.

"I know how to make a bed. I've been doing it for a lot of years." He grinned. "Once in a while, anyway." With his hand on the back of her neck, he stopped grinning and pressed his mouth to hers. His other hand slid up under her blue knit top. Her breasts were confined within a brassiere and he cupped his hand around one well-filled cup.

Torey was startled by the degree of excitement he was inciting again. Apparently what they'd started today wasn't going to die a sudden death.

The thought made her exceedingly happy. Curling her fingers into his hair, Torey let all of the good feelings flow through her. Bart's hand on her breast felt like it was right where it belonged, and his lips on hers felt like pure heaven. Her blood was racing again by the time they stopped kissing.

"Are you still afraid of me?"

Torey put her fingertips on his mouth, tenderly tracing the contour of his bottom lip. She smiled. "A little."

"You shouldn't be, not after today."

"Maybe I should be even *more* afraid of you after today."

"Why do you say that?"

Torey gave a small laugh, a nervous reaction to the topic. Bart removed his hand from under her top and she sat up straighter. "I . . . can't help wondering where this might be going," she admitted. "Do you know?"

"I've been thinking about it." Bart's expression had become very sober, slightly guarded. "I know you don't just fall into bed with every guy that comes along."

"No, I don't," she confirmed quietly.

"Why me, Torey?"

"I told you before that I was drawn to you." Torey got up, and Bart didn't try to stop her. She sat in the next chair and looked off at the same scene Bart had been admiring earlier. "I don't understand it any better than you do," she said softly. "That day I came to your house..."

"That's when it started?"

Torey nodded. "I know how you feel about a—" she couldn't quite bring herself to say wife "—serious relationship."

"Do you?" Bart looked unconvinced. "Torey, I'm going to see that Rob and Rich get the education they want if it means working seven days a week for the next ten years."

"I know."

"I don't have the time, the money or the energy for a serious relationship." The content of his own words suddenly struck Bart. What was he saying? What did he expect from Torey? She didn't deserve this kind of treatment. Not her. Torey deserved much more than he could ever give her. Torey deserved a...a Steve Johnson! Oh, he knew full well who Steve Johnson was, despite the little games he played with Torey about the veterinarian's name. Dr. Johnson was a nice enough, very steady guy who was earning himself a good reputation and, no doubt, a damned good living in the area.

"Damn," Bart muttered, lunging out of the chair, shaken by the conclusion he'd reached.

"What's wrong?" Torey's startled eyes followed his erratic pacing. "Bart?"

He stopped and looked at her, and Torey's heart sank clear to her toes at the expression on his face. "I think it would be best if we broke this little romance up right now," Bart said coolly.

"*What?*"

"You heard me. You'll end up getting hurt, and believe it or not, I don't want that any more than you do. Maybe less."

Torey slowly rose from the chair. "And I have no say in the matter? Suppose I'm willing to take the risk?"

"You want an affair? I don't believe that, Torey. You're not cut out for that kind of thing."

"Don't be so sure! Bart—"

"Can you look me in the eye and tell me you're not thinking of something serious in the back of your mind?"

Color flooded Torey's face. Her reply was a hastily stammered, "Things change. Who knows what might happen next week, next month?"

"Nothing's going to change. My brothers and I are going to work our tails off every summer on that mountain. They're going to go away in the fall and return in the spring. For years, Torey, for up to ten years."

Torey dropped her eyes. "I honestly didn't know that Rob and Rich were so...dedicated."

"Well, you know it now. Sure, they've raised a little hell. So have I. The Scanlons have a reputation. I know all about it and it doesn't bother me that much. But it would bother the hell out of me if the local gossips included you in their exaggerated stories. They're not going to get the chance. I'm going to stay away from you, Torey."

What had been born in passion today was now trying to die inside Torey. She fought against it, allowing anger and bitterness to sweep through her. The last man she would ever have thought to possess noble impulses was destroying her, and it was he who had just given her life!

"How dare you make a unilateral decision about this!" Her gray eyes were black with fury. "If you want nothing more to do with me, just come right out and say so. But don't give me that sanctimonious drivel about wanting to protect me from gossip!''

A heavy silence stretched while they glared at each other. "Is that what you really think, that I made all that up for a reason to stay away from you?" Bart took a forward step. "Let me ask you something, Torey. If that were the case, if I really didn't want anything further between us, do you think I'd hesitate to say so?"

She knew he wouldn't. Bart had never been afraid to say anything. Who knew that better than her?

Tears filled her eyes. "Then, for God's sake, don't do this." A strange and unfamiliar pain ripped at Torey's insides. Why was she pleading a case she wasn't even sure she wanted to win? Hadn't she been going around and around with herself on how often lightning could strike in the same place? Bart was as ambiguous about it as she was, but forgetting every speck of pride wasn't going to suddenly change circumstances.

Bart's jaw clenched and he looked away from her tears. He couldn't be weak about this. They had no future together, and he wasn't going to sneak around and humiliate Torey with an affair that would be all over the county before either of them even realized it. He shouldn't have pushed her into going to bed with him today. He should have listened to the conscience that had labeled Torey the kind of woman men married.

But . . . he'd wanted her so damn much.

He still did.

Shaking off the debilitating thoughts, Bart ran a weary hand over his face and hair. "I'm going to go. Forget today. You'll be better off not thinking about it."

Through a layer of blurring tears, Torey watched him walk toward his pickup. Then her pulse quickened. Bart had turned around and was coming back. "Did you order the poplars yet?"

"No," she whispered.

"Do it. See if Joe will deliver them this week. The twins and I will put them in next weekend."

Torey just stared at him. He waited a moment, then turned away and climbed into his truck. The motor roared to life, and in a minute, he was gone.

Dazed, Torey stumbled to a chair and fell into it. She was still there when Lorna arrived an hour later.

The older woman called a cheery "Hi, Torey" as she got out of the car.

"Hi, Lorna."

Lorna crossed the yard to the patio. Her smile vanished. "What's wrong?"

Torey knew that this was something she didn't want to talk about with anyone, not even Lorna. "Nothing, really. I was just about to go in. How was dinner with the Kendricks?"

Lorna looked suspicious, but she went along with Torey. "Wonderful, as always. Did you eat?"

"No. Maybe I'll have a piece of that chicken now." The thought of food wasn't exactly thrilling, but Torey knew she had to try to eat or Lorna would never let her alone.

"You look kind of peaked. Do you feel all right?"

Torey grabbed at the excuse. "I've had a bit of a headache all day." It wasn't a complete lie.

They walked into the house. "You said on the phone you were going out this afternoon," Lorna persisted.

"Oh, yes. I forgot I had mentioned that. I ended up staying home. Bart asked me to go to Billings for supper, and I was undecided for a while. But this headache..."

"I see. Well, you'll probably feel much better if you eat."

Torey forced a faint smile. "No doubt."

Nine

Torey wanted very much to be broadminded about Bart's attitude. But try as she might, she was much more emotionally bruised from Sunday afternoon than she'd initially realized, and it was impossible to disassociate herself from the entanglement enough to be very generous. It was entirely feasible—painful as the prospect was—that once Bart had gotten what he'd wanted from her, he had no further interest. He was a sharp-minded man, certainly clever enough to use his commitment to his twin brothers to wriggle out of a situation he found uncomfortable or crowding. He'd confronted her head-on when she'd accused him of doing that, but Bart had always been good with words and his strong defense could have been just another ploy.

Underlying the entire episode were feelings, her own and those she'd picked up from Bart. Or those she'd *thought* she had picked up. Maybe she was mistaken there, too.

It was all very discouraging. And heartbreaking. Torey didn't imagine herself in love with Bart Scanlon, but her emotions had been deeply ruffled ever since she'd gone to the Scanlon house to discuss the road. Making love the way they had was no small matter to her, and something in Torey told her she would never quite get over it, never quite be the same person she'd been before it had happened.

Bart's suggestion—or rather, demand—that she order the poplars so he and the twins could set them out on the weekend stuck in Torey's craw. As he wanted no further contact between them, she wondered if it wouldn't be best to just forget about Bart participating in the poplar project. She could pay the full cost of the trees herself, eliminating any need to even speak to Bart again. They had coexisted for years with very little personal interaction, and with some effort, could easily fall back into that pattern. It didn't seem the best course, to her, to delay the complete break by spending a weekend together planting trees.

By Wednesday morning Torey still hadn't called Joe Holcombe, the local greenhouse and tree-farm owner. She was outside, working in the garden, when she heard a vehicle on her driveway and looked up from the small weeds she was hoeing out from between two rows of carrots. A large truck lumbered up beside the house and stopped. Its bed was full of poplar trees.

Torey straightened her back slowly. *She* hadn't ordered the trees and Lorna wouldn't do it without a request from Torey, which meant Bart had taken it upon himself to have the poplars delivered. Torey tensed with immediate anger. How dare he presume so much? Bart was too damned bossy. Look how he had railed at her about riding Nero, just because the horse was a stallion and hard to handle! She had been riding horses all of her life and didn't need Bart Scanlon sticking his nose in and deciding which ones she should avoid.

Nor did she need him doing something she'd been deliberately procrastinating on, ordering those trees!

Containing her resentment, Torey walked out to meet the driver of the truck, who had climbed down from the cab and spotted her. It wasn't Joe, but she knew the young man. "Hello, Brock."

"Hi, Torey. How've you been?"

"Fine, thanks."

"Got a nice load of Russian Poplars here."

"I see that."

"Where do you want them unloaded?"

A strong urge to tell Joe Holcombe's young employee that she didn't want the poplars unloaded at all lay on the tip of Torey's tongue. But then she wondered if she wasn't being petty. She really did feel that the trees were necessary eventually. Men were laying gravel on Bart's road now, and already gusts of wind had brought whirling clouds of dust toward her house. Nothing major yet, but when logging trucks started using the road, dust could be a problem.

Lorna came out of the house. "Oh, I didn't know you had ordered the trees, Torey. Hello, Brock."

"Hi, Lorna."

"How's your mother? I haven't seen her for several weeks now."

While Lorna and Brock chatted, Torey walked around the truck and took a look at the trees. They were good stock, large and healthy-looking, exactly what she would have ordered. It galled her that Bart had interfered. He must have noticed that no trees had been delivered to the Lancaster ranch. Bart could have called her to find out what was going on, but he had obviously called Joe instead.

What she should do is call Bart and give him a piece of her mind, the damned busybody!

By the time Torey made a complete circle of the truck, she knew she wasn't going to call Bart, even though he deserved a tongue-lashing. The trees were here, and nothing would be gained by screaming at Bart or anyone else.

"Put them along the fence, Brock," Torey told the young man. "Do you need some help with the unloading? I could go find Dex to give you a hand." Dex Cotter was Torey's current hired man, and he was out in the south pasture changing the location of some irrigation pipes.

"Nope. I've got tree-unloading down to a science," Brock said with a confident laugh, and he got to work.

After a few minutes, Lorna returned to the house. Torey watched Brock a little longer, then seeing that unloading twenty-two trees was going to take a while, she started back to the garden.

"Torey? Telephone," Lorna called out the back door. "It's Steve."

Torey felt a flash of impatience, then chided herself. It wasn't Steve's fault that she was so down in the dumps. On the way in, Torey realized that she couldn't keep on seeing Steve. Even if she and Bart never again went any further than a restrained hello, she couldn't hurt Steve by letting him hope that their dates might go somewhere.

Pausing before picking up the phone, Torey knew what she had to do: See Steve once more and tell him she was emotionally involved with someone else.

It was the painfully precise truth.

It was after seven p.m. before Bart had time to inspect the road that day. He was dirty, sweaty and exhausted, but he wanted to check the road's progress before he went home. He'd fully intended on passing Torey's house without even slowing down, but the small forest of trees in wooden containers along her side of the fence was impossible to miss.

He stopped the pickup and got out, walking over to the fence to take a look at the poplars. He'd called Joe Holcombe on Tuesday to ask when he was going to deliver Torey Lancaster's order, wanting to get the job of planting them over and done with during the upcoming weekend. Joe's insistence that Torey hadn't placed the order had rankled the hell out of Bart. His logging trucks would be using the road within a week, and he didn't want Torey griping and complaining because she had to look at the traffic. "Deliver the trees, Joe. I don't know why Torey hasn't called you, but I'll take full responsibility for the order."

They were good-looking trees, Bart had to admit, taller than he was in their boxes. Set out, they'd be just about his height.

He started back to his pickup, then looked across the fence again. A light blue Wagoneer was driving up to Torey's house. Bart froze, recognizing the man getting out. It was Steve Johnson, obviously here to pick up Torey for the evening.

A bitter taste rose in Bart's throat, while the muscles in his body tensed. Judging the veterinarian as a better choice than he was for Torey Lancaster was a hell of a lot easier to deal with when Steve wasn't around, Bart realized. What he'd like to do is hop the fence and kick the vet's butt clear into the next county!

He had no right to be sick with jealousy, though, no right at all. It was his own doing that it wasn't him picking up Torey tonight.

Bart shook his head. He was too damned tired to be picking anyone up tonight. He'd done the right thing in breaking off with Torey, and if he got an ache in the gut every time he saw her with another man, he'd just have to learn to live with it.

Steve had gone to the front door and someone had let him in. Bart was about to turn his back on the whole scene when the door opened again and Steve and Torey came out. She was dressed in black and white, and Bart's mouth was suddenly dusty-dry. In the long rays of the setting sun her auburn hair was more red than brown. She was utterly beautiful, the embodiment of womankind. He knew he was staring, but he was still stunned when Torey looked his way and caught him.

She stopped dead in her tracks and stared back, and for the barest fraction of time, there was only the two of them on the planet. Bart saw her chin lift slightly, a subtly defiant movement, then she turned and hurried to the Wagoneer.

"Torey!" Bart startled himself by yelling her name, and from Torey's reaction, he'd startled her, too. He saw her say something to Steve, then walk toward the fence.

"You called?" she said in a saccharine tone.

Bart was seldom at a loss for words, but his mind was suddenly a blank. Torey laid a hand on the fence post within reach. "What do you want, Bart?"

Awkwardly he gestured to the trees. "I was just looking at the poplars. They seem fine to me. How do they look to you?"

Her eyes narrowed. "You ordered them, didn't you?"

"You wanted them."

"I was going to call Joe. You didn't have to interfere."

Bart cocked an eyebrow. "Is that what I did?"

"What would you call it?"

"You're hard to please." His voice dropped. "Not with everything, though. There's one area..."

A slow flush crept up Torey's neck and face. There was no mistaking the "area" Bart was referring to. He'd pleased her in bed, and he wasn't above reminding her of it. To what purpose, though? Why refresh a memory that he'd told her to forget? "You do have a nerve, don't you?" she said in a harsh undertone, angry that after his rather cruel dismissal Sunday afternoon, he seemed to want to keep her aware of the day's events.

"I always did, Torey."

"Yes, you always did," she agreed derisively. Torey glanced back at the Wagoneer. Steve was sitting behind the wheel. "Why did you call me over here?" she demanded, turning back to Bart. "You must have had a better reason than these trees."

For the first time in twenty years Torey saw a glimmer of embarrassment on Bart's face. He hadn't had a reason at all. He'd seen her leaving with Steve and had decided to intrude.

And then it came to her. Seeing her going off with Steve *was* the reason for Bart's intrusion. Bart didn't like it, and he simply wasn't a man who could stand by and do nothing about something he didn't like.

A rush of words clogged Torey's throat, an aching desire to explain why she was seeing Steve tonight. It would be very easy to soothe the strain that she now realized was quite apparent in Bart's eyes. An explanation would require only a few simple phrases, but how dare he look at her with a soulful, accusing expression? How dare he remind her of their lovemaking when he'd been so insensitive afterward?

He still wanted her. Torey could see it in his eyes and feel it in her heart. Something gladdened within her, even while she felt the stinging hopelessness of a man and woman wanting one another and denying it.

"I've got to go," she said dully, spiritless over the futile situation.

"Have a good time."

Again the urge to set Bart straight about the upcoming evening gnawed at Torey. But there was a certain justice in him suffering a little. Since Sunday, she'd endured her share of anguish, and if it hurt him to watch her drive off with Steve, maybe he deserved it.

Still, she couldn't quite bring herself to make a flippant reply. Telling him she fully intended to would be a lie. She wasn't looking forward to the evening in the least. Explaining to Steve that she thought it best to terminate their friendship was far from a pleasant prospect. The only thing that made it any less heartless than what Bart had done to her was the fact that she had never given Steve any reason to hope for anything serious from her.

"I've got to go," Torey repeated quietly, and turned and walked back to the Wagoneer. Steve started it immediately.

When it was gone, heading for the highway, Bart felt drained, mentally, emotionally and physically. He climbed behind the wheel of his pickup and stared off down the new road without really seeing it. Sunday afternoon's events filled his brain, Torey naked, Torey wild-eyed and dazed with passion, Torey's mouth, her beautiful body, her response to him, Torey...Torey...Torey. Bart's stomach churned while desire tormented his loins.

This was more than simple lust, wasn't it? Yes, he thought of Torey in sexual terms, but when had he ever cared if the woman he was seeing dated someone else? He'd never once tried to maintain a one-on-one relationship; it simply hadn't mattered if he was the only man in a woman's life.

Lord, did it matter that much now? Apparently it didn't to Torey. If she'd had any feelings for him beyond the physical attraction she'd admitted to, she'd certainly gotten over them fast. Three days after making love with him, she was out with Steve.

To do what? She'd proclaimed them only friends several times, but Bart couldn't relate to that sort of relationship between a beautiful, sensual woman like Torey and any man with a normal, healthy appetite for the opposite sex. Bart didn't know the veterinarian all that well, but Steve Johnson didn't strike him as at all *un*healthy.

Releasing a long, discouraged sigh, Bart started the pickup. Regardless of logic and common sense, Torey Lancaster was again in his system. More so now than ever. Torey might have been able to put Sunday behind her without a backward glance, but he'd opened himself up for some sleepless nights.

Bart grinned cynically. Sleepless nights? As tired as he was when he crawled into bed at night, even Torey Lancaster's abundant charms didn't have the power to keep him awake. But there were few moments during the day when she was very far from his thoughts.

Torey heard Lorna talking on the telephone Friday afternoon when she came in for dinner. "She just walked through the door, Bart. I'll put her on."

Bart? Torey's pulse came alive. She hadn't even seen Bart near the new road since Wednesday evening, and the memory of his strange behavior that night had been keeping Torey on pins and needles. She stood by anxiously, waiting for Lorna to hand over the phone.

"All right, I'll tell her. Goodbye." Lorna put the phone down. "Bart said to tell you that he and the twins will be over tomorrow afternoon to start on those trees."

Torey could hardly believe he'd relayed the message through Lorna when *she'd* been standing right there. "Apparently he didn't want to talk to me."

Lorna gave her a curious look. "Apparently not."

The slight was almost more than she could take, but Torey tried to appear unaffected. "Dinner smells good. I'll go wash up."

"Do you have a date tonight?"

"No, no date."

Lorna went to the oven and peeked in. "No Steve, no Bart. Hmmm."

"Hmmm, what, Lorna?"

"Nothing. Just hmmm."

Torey realized she couldn't keep everything from Lorna. Until this thing with Bart, she'd kept nothing from her longtime companion. Torey opened the refrigerator and took out the pitcher of iced tea. "I told Steve last Wednesday night that I wouldn't be seeing him anymore."

"Oh?"

Torey filled a glass with tea. "It's not fair to date a man and watch him becoming more interested in you when you don't reciprocate his feelings."

"I see. You don't reciprocate Steve's feelings."

"No, I don't. Steve's a very nice man, Lorna. I didn't want him hurt by something I can't help."

"And Bart?"

Torey stared blankly. "What does Bart have to do with Steve?"

"Well, you were explaining why you don't have a date tonight, and I thought we were talking about both Steve and Bart."

"*I* wasn't."

"Oh, sorry. Guess I misunderstood."

Lorna was busily getting dinner on the table. Torey watched her a moment, then mumbled, "I better go wash up." Hurrying from the kitchen, she knew she couldn't blame Lorna for wondering what was going on with her and Bart. When he made it so plain that he didn't even want to talk to her on the phone, Lorna was bound to have questions.

Now that Torey thought about Bart's snub, it made her angry. Actually, come tomorrow, she just might tell him about several things he'd done lately that had made her angry. Having those trees delivered still made her see red, and then spying on her when Steve picked her up was really low.

But he really hadn't been spying, had he? Torey bit her lip hard while she washed her hands in the bathroom sink. He'd been there because of the road, not because of her, and he'd looked darned shaky because she was going off with Steve, as though that was the last thing he would have hoped to see.

Torey could still feel the weight of that moment when they'd looked long and hard at each other. There'd been something rather earthshaking about that exchanged look, the strangest sense of alliance. But it had been brief and then she'd sensed something else: disapproval. Bart was like a damned dog in a manger; he didn't want her, but he didn't want Steve Johnson to have her, either.

Well, he needn't worry about Steve anymore, although what Bart might think about her dating Steve hadn't had a thing to do with why she'd broken off the friendship. Torey had been completely honest with Lorna about Steve. She'd known for some time that Steve was hoping their relationship would develop into more than it was, and even without Bart in the picture, Torey knew it would never happen.

No, she had nothing to be ashamed of where Steve was concerned. She'd been very forthright with him right from the onset. True, she'd been content dating him until Bart had slammed into her life, but she'd never given Steve any reason to expect more than friendship from her.

Torey washed her face, dried it and applied some lotion to her skin. While she brushed her hair, she thought of tomorrow afternoon. Just how was Bart going to keep from talking to her while he and the twins were planting those trees?

She frowned. Bart would *have* to talk to her tomorrow, but if he reverted to his old habit of taunts and gibes, she would brain him, and do it in front of the twins and Lorna, too, if that's what it took.

Enough was enough. Maybe there was nothing in the future for Torey Lancaster and Bart Scanlon other than the accident of owning adjoining ranches. Maybe she would someday even reach the point of looking at last Sunday with only fond memories instead of the knot in her stomach she'd been living with. But no way, under no circumstances, was she going to put up with Bart's former brand of derision.

Ten

The smell of tangy herbs and spices filled the house. Strolling into the kitchen, Torey sniffed appreciatively. "What are you cooking, Lorna?"

"Spaghetti sauce."

"Oh, great! You haven't made Italian spaghetti in ages." Torey picked up the cover of the large pot and peeked inside. "Smells heavenly, but you've got enough here to feed an army."

Lorna smiled sheepishly. "Well, I thought with the Scanlons working here all afternoon, maybe we should feed them dinner. Only if you agree, of course," she added hastily.

How could she refuse? Torey thought wryly. Besides, she'd asked Dex Cotter, her hired man, to work that afternoon, too, and she knew very well that Dex was a bachelor and would be delighted with an invitation to indulge in one of Lorna's home-cooked meals. But Torey didn't want to force that kind of social issue with Bart, not with so many ambiguities going on between them. "That's fine," she agreed soberly. "But *you* ask them."

Lorna smiled brightly. "I'll be glad to do the asking."

Torey was on edge all morning, anticipating Bart's arrival with alternating hot and cold flashes. One minute she assumed a haughty, go-to-hell expression, preparing it ahead of time for her arrogant neighbor, and the next minute relented into a sickish smile, which reflected a little more accurately her true state of mind.

Twice she went out with the garden hose and sprayed the trees. Brock had instructed her to keep them damp. "Not sopping wet, Torey. But make sure the ground around the roots never gets dried out."

All in all, the morning passed with more aimless wandering than anything productive. The image of Bart within reach all afternoon, and maybe even staying for dinner, was excruciatingly unnerving. By noon Torey was too unsettled to eat more than a few bites, although she did her best to hold up her end of a casual conversation with Lorna during the meal.

The day was bright and hot enough that Torey had put on shorts and a sleeveless top. She planned to help out where she could with the tree-planting, but she suspected that with four men on the project, there would be little for her to do. If nothing else, though, she would keep the workers supplied with lemonade and iced tea, which Lorna had prepared gallons of.

At one o'clock Dex arrived, and a few minutes later the Scanlons drove up. Behind Bart's black pickup was a flatbed trailer carrying a small tractor with a backhoe attachment. Everyone said hello. Bart was wearing his dark glasses, concealing whatever he might be thinking about being thrust into her presence, Torey noted. She pasted on a who-cares expression and did a little concealing of her own. Bart Scanlon would forever affect her, she admitted again. She felt his long, lanky body and dark, charismatic aura in every cell of her being.

The twins walked around and inspected the trees until Bart said, "Let's get the tractor unloaded, boys." Dex went to the toolshed for shovels and a bag of the fertilizer Torey had recently purchased. "Have you given any thought to the exact placement of the trees?" Bart asked her.

Torey nodded and walked over to the fence. "I've put in small stakes, marking each spot." It seemed very strange for the two of them to be talking as though nothing intimate had ever occurred. Bart was playing the good neighbor role today, she realized with a touch of resentment. He didn't appear to be the least bit uncomfortable, and that didn't seem quite fair to Torey.

Bart had followed, and he nodded approvingly at the neat row of stakes along the fence. "Good. To start with, Rob will run the tractor and dig the initial holes. Rich will finish rounding them out with a shovel. They can trade off on those jobs after a while and Dex and I will set the trees. The whole thing shouldn't take more than a few hours."

"You're very organized." Torey had tried to keep her tone emotionless, but a hint of sarcasm had colored it, just the same.

"I'd like to get it over and done with."

The blunt statement sounded like the period at the end of a long sentence, like the end of a book, like the irrevocable finish to something. Stung by the conclusiveness in Bart's voice, Torey looked away. "Yes, I'm sure you would."

"Not because of what you're thinking, Torey."

She brought her gaze back to him, weary of what was beginning to feel like a game of cat and mouse. "What am I thinking, Bart?" She wished she could see his eyes, because the question had been daring, challenging, and all of his emotion was hidden from her by black lenses.

He hesitated, then shook his head. "I'm not going to get into that kind of discussion with you."

"You started it."

"My mistake." Bart walked off.

Torey felt her veneer cracking. He still had the power to destroy her with a few words, even if they weren't the old wisecracks from the past. Her eyes burned, and she blinked hard to keep the tears back.

The next hour was a blur of activity. Torey and Lorna kept the men supplied with cool drinks. Rob and Rich tossed their shirts first, but finally Bart and Dex stripped down, too. One by one, the trees were planted. But it wasn't the splendor of the poplars Torey kept casting turmoil-laden glances at; it was the splendor of Bart Scanlon.

Because the sun was so glaring, Torey had gone into the house for her own sunglasses and a straw hat. The dark glasses and wide hat brim allowed her the freedom to look where she wanted to, and she deliberately used the opportunity to study Bart.

Rob and Rich Scanlon were handsome young men, but their older brother beat them by a mile. Along with his good looks, Bart's grace and economy of movement were mesmerizing. Torey narrowed her eyes in thought. It was so futile to keep on feeling things for Bart. In all honesty, she should despise him. Why didn't she? For years and years she hadn't been able to drum up anything for Bart *but* an intense and abiding dislike, and now, when she had a much more substantial reason for hating him, she only wanted to touch him, to experience his kisses again. Was she mad?

Torey sighed. She wasn't mad, or even slightly on the brink of madness. She was half in love with the big jerk, that was her problem.

The thought weakened Torey's knees. She was leaning against the front fender of Bart's pickup, and for a moment she felt like sinking to the ground. In love with Bart Scanlon? Lord, she *must* be mad!

"We need some more fertilizer," Bart announced.

Dex was tamping the last of the bag and some dirt around the trunk of the tree he and Bart had just planted. Rob was on the tractor, working down the line, and Rich was wielding a shovel, preparing a hole for another tree. Torey pushed away from the pickup's fender. "I'll show you where it is." The bags were fifty pounds each, too heavy for her to carry.

She walked quickly, leading the way to the toolshed. Torey opened the door and stepped inside of the small building. "In that corner," she pointed out. Bart brushed past her, heading for the designated spot in the shed.

It occurred to Torey that they were alone, and an impulse she couldn't banish took hold of her. Deliberately, she closed the door and leaned against it. The shed was instantly dim and shadowy. Bart turned, surprise on his face. "What did you do that for?"

Torey's mouth and throat had gone dry. "I . . . I'm not sure." She saw him remove his dark glasses, and she reached up slowly and took off her own glasses. They stared at each other and Torey's tension mounted until she thought she might scream. Bart's unblinking scrutiny wasn't unkind, but it was deeply, searingly penetrating.

"Why did you close the door, Torey?"

She swallowed. Her face was burning, but then, so was her body. She didn't want to give up every vestige of pride with Bart, and she wondered if this woman standing here was really Torey Lancaster. When had she changed so much? At what precise moment had she become a woman who could challenge a man who was determined to maintain a breach between them?

Bart advanced, a dark scowl on his face. "You can't leave it alone, can you? How many men do you need?"

"What?" She didn't have the slightest inkling of what he was talking about, and the word conveyed how effectively he'd stunned her.

"Johnson, me. Do you need both of us?"

She understood then, remembering Wednesday evening. The explanation she had wanted to offer that evening surfaced and taunted. Bart had an erroneous perception of the event, which was understandable, given the circumstances. Torey's words were shaky. "Going out with Steve last Wednesday wasn't what you're thinking."

Bart used her own words on her. "What am I thinking, Torey?"

She didn't know what to say. She was behaving like a fool and just begging to be emotionally crushed. Tears filled her eyes. "I'm sorry," she whispered huskily, and turned to open the door.

Something snapped in Bart, and he rushed forward and took her in his arms. Torey's hat fell to the floor. With his jaw clenched, Bart held her head to the strong heartbeat in his chest with a hand in her hair. He'd wanted to do this from the moment he'd arrived, even longer than that. Since Wednesday evening, when he'd seen her go off with Steve Johnson, Bart had been wracked with crazy urges.

She felt so good, so soft and warm and womanly. Her breasts, her rigid little nipples, were burning two holes in his bare chest. He felt his body coming alive and desire streaking through him, but even more influencing was the desire he felt in Torey. She seemed to be melting against him, molding around every dip and curve he possessed, and her hands slid up his chest. "Oh, Bart," she whispered.

He looked down, and her lips were turned up to him, slightly parted, inviting, asking. With a groan he took them. His mouth was rough, demanding, punishing. How could he stay away from her if she did things like closing them off from the rest of the world in a dark toolshed?

Would she seek other opportunities for them to be alone? He was only human, dammit!

His hands were roaming, finding her breasts, remembering the seductive female curves of her body. One hand sought bare skin and slipped up under the hem of her blouse. Her tongue was even bolder than his, moving in his mouth, unmercifully tormenting him. They were both breathing hard, taking air in harsh-sounding gasps. Her shorts had a front zipper, and he caught the tab and yanked it down.

Dazed, dizzy from a head full of erotic images, and feeling like she could make love to this man forever, Torey groped just as heedlessly. Her fingertips absorbed the sensually exciting masculine slopes and contours of strong muscles and hot skin. She lingered at the hair on his chest, but then left it for an even more tantalizing portion of Bart's body. Her hand opened on his fly and then felt around for the top of his zipper.

They could make love right here in this musty little shed, Bart realized, with the sound of the tractor and the voices of Rob, Rich and Dex as background music. Lord, if they only could! He was on fire, almost beyond control.

But they couldn't. They'd already been gone too long. Dex needed the fertilizer. He could come looking for it at any minute.

Bart took both of her hands in his and held them between them. "Not here," he whispered unsteadily.

She was unzipped, he was partially unzipped. Her face was flushed, he knew that his had to be. "Where, then?" she whispered back.

"Torey..." His voice was anguished. He'd tried to do the right thing and it wasn't working. They were both asking for heartache, but how did a man turn his back on a woman he'd wanted his entire life?

"Meet me somewhere," she urged. "Tonight, Bart."

"Where?"

Torey glanced around, as if there were an answer some-where in the dusky little shed. She didn't want to go where there might be people. She wanted them to be alone. Com-pletely alone. But where was there such a place? As Bart had said, he had the twins and she had Lorna.

Her shoulders slumped. "I don't know."

Bart reached down and slowly pulled the zipper up on her shorts. "I'll pick you up around eight."

Their gazes locked for a long moment, and then yank-ing his own zipper up, he went over to the bags of fertilizer in the corner. As easily as if he were picking up feathers, he hoisted the heavy bag to one shoulder. "Open the door for me," he said quietly.

She complied, and then stood back. He stopped right in front of her. "I hope you know what you're doing," he said, his tone husky and weighted with uncertainty. "I'm not sure I do."

She swallowed. "I hope so, too, Bart."

"You're all invited to dinner tonight," Lorna an-nounced when the four men took a break. Rob and Rich grinned. "I hope you like spaghetti," Lorna added.

"Lorna only makes the best sauce in the western hemi-sphere," Torey boasted.

Bart laughed. "The Scanlons will eat anything that doesn't eat them first. Thanks, Lorna. I'm sure I can speak for these two perpetually hungry hombres here. We'd all three appreciate a good meal."

Lorna looked slightly undone, which Torey caught. The older woman had already made several comments to the effect that Rob and Rich Scanlon were good workers and maybe not as bad as she'd heard. "I think you called them scamps," Torey had dryly reminded.

"Well, they're really only motherless boys, aren't they? Bart seems to have done a good job, considering."

Torey could see what was cooking behind Lorna's eyes because of Bart's "perpetually hungry hombres" comment: Those poor boys weren't getting enough of the right kind of food!

Well, they'd get filled up tonight. Not only was there enough spaghetti sauce to feed three times the people on the Lancaster place, Lorna had baked three apple pies and a chocolate cake.

With the dinner plans settled, Lorna went back to the house. Torey stayed out a little longer, then decided to go in and at least set the table. Lorna had been busy in the kitchen most of the day, while Torey's biggest contribution had been the delivery of lemonade and iced tea. She was almost to the house when she heard a sudden yelp and a yell from behind her.

Startled, she looked back to see Bart lunging over to where Rich was lying on the ground. Rob was scrambling off of the tractor and Dex was standing deathly still, holding a shovel, looking as pale as a ghost. "What happened?" she called, running back to the men.

"Oh, Lord," she said when she saw that Rich's forehead was bleeding.

Dex mumbled, "Damn, I'm sorry. Rich, you raised up just as I swung this here shovel."

Bart glanced up at Torey. "Get some wet towels."

"Yes, of course." Torey dashed to the house. "Make an ice pack, Lorna. Rich got hit on the forehead with Dex's shovel."

"Oh, my goodness!" Lorna yanked the freezer door open on the refrigerator while Torey grabbed two kitchen towels and soaked them with water at the sink. With the wet towels she raced back outside.

Bart took one and pressed it to Rich's forehead. Torey had gotten a good look at the blood spurting from the cut, and her stomach turned over.

"I'm okay," Rich mumbled, trying to sit up.

"Lie still," Bart gruffly commanded, and the lanky boy laid back down. Rob slid to the ground beside his twin brother, his eyes darting from Rich to Bart. Neither spoke, but Torey saw that there were all kinds of communication in the visual exchange.

Dex hadn't moved and looked paler than Rich did. Torey glanced at the hired man and gave him a small, encouraging smile. "It was an accident, Dex," she said softly.

Her gaze returned to the three Scanlons. Shirtless, so very much alike in looks, there was something acutely special about their communion, Torey realized. One of them was injured, and the other two felt it as strongly as if it were themselves. The bond among the three brothers was almost tangible. The love between them was unquestionable, maybe the most moving display of familial oneness that Torey had ever witnessed.

It shook her. She remembered her doubts about the twins' career expectations, and yes, she'd been harboring some resentment that Bart had used his brothers as an excuse to stay away from her. She hadn't wanted to believe it, but it was true, wasn't it? Bart was willing to deny himself anything to do what he felt was best for his brothers.

Shame that she had thrown herself at Bart in the toolshed washed over Torey in a dizzying wave. He had given up his education and dream of becoming a doctor so the twins wouldn't be uprooted and sent to foster homes; he had worked hard for ten years to raise his brothers, and, he certainly wasn't going to let a woman deter him from finishing the job.

All she could ever expect from Bart Scanlon was the affair he'd decided she wasn't cut out for. It was a sad summation of the situation, but Torey knew as certainly as she drew breath that it was right on the mark.

Bart lifted the towel. Torey could see that the cut was a serious injury. "All right," Bart declared. "We're going to the hospital."

Lorna ran up. "Here's an ice bag, Bart."

"Thanks." He took the ice bag from Lorna and the other towel from Torey. After exchanging the towels on Rich's forehead, he pressed the ice bag to the spot. "Hold it there, Rich." Bart got to his feet, and he and Rob helped Rich stand up. They made their way to Bart's pickup. When the boys were settled in the cab, Bart came back to the concerned trio standing by the tractor.

"Dex, you look worse than Rich. It was an accident, man. A few stitches and Rich will be as good as new."

"I'm sure sorry about it, Bart."

"I know you are." Bart gathered up his and the twins' shirts and returned to the pickup. "See you all later," he called.

Torey, Lorna and Dex watched the pickup speeding down the driveway. Accidents happened on ranches. Tools, animals and people sometimes collided through mistiming, a misstep, or, in some cases, carelessness. Torey hadn't seen Rich and Dex's collision, but Dex was a responsible man and even Bart had told him it had been purely accidental. At any rate, Dex didn't look as though he'd relish going back to work. Torey's spirits weren't the best, either, and Lorna's pleasant face was deeply furrowed with worry. Clearly, planting any more trees was out for today.

"We'll call it quits for the day," Torey announced.

Dex nodded solemnly. "Yeah, I think that's best." He brought the shovel he was still holding over to the tractor and stood it against the side of the machine. "I'll pick up these tools before I leave."

"No, you go ahead, Dex. I'll take care of the tools."

Lorna spoke up. "Come in the house and I'll give you some spaghetti sauce to take home for your dinner, Dex."

"Thanks, Lorna." Dex followed Lorna to the house.

Alone, Torey walked over to the trees that had just been planted. Nine of the poplars were in the ground, which left thirteen still in wooden boxes. Torey could see that the row of trees was going to be an attractive break between the Lancaster and Scanlon ranches, but did she really need it? She glanced across the fence to the road that had started everything.

She'd been a complainer and not very nice about that road, she admitted. And was it really that bad? If it had been someone other than Bart putting it in, would she have been so demanding about it? Bart had always been such an irritant, and had she seen and taken an opportunity to hassle him for a change?

Torey realized she wasn't very proud of that possibility. She had it very easy compared to Bart's role in life. Would she have done as well as he had if it had been her left alone with eight-year-old twin brothers at twenty years of age?

Yes, his house was a mess, but hers wouldn't be so perfectly kept without Lorna. It was Lorna's constant attention, not hers, that made the Lancaster house a real home. Other than caring for her bedroom, Torey knew how little she did in the house. She would much rather go out with Dex and repair fences, move cattle from one pasture to another, put up hay, relocate irrigation pipes, tend the garden, do almost anything else to avoid housework.

She'd been quick to find fault with Bart's housekeeping. She'd also come very close to ridiculing his intentions to help Rob and Rich through a medical education.

But now she felt differently. Through narrowed, thoughtful eyes, Torey stared off across Scanlon land. Bart's cattle were scattered here and there throughout the enormous pasture, creating a peaceful scene that didn't quite reach Torey's troubled soul.

She should leave him alone, she thought with a profound sadness. Tempting him into a serious relationship would be callous, maybe the most selfish thing she'd ever done. And Bart was right about one thing: She wasn't cut out for an affair. Incredible sex and feelings of love meant permanency to her, and permanency meant marriage, babies, growing old together. That scenario wasn't in Bart's plans.

"Damn," Torey whispered, and wiped away a tear that had escaped a corner of one eye.

Just in time, too, because Dex came up behind her. "What do you think, Torey? Will Bart want to finish this job tomorrow?" Dex was carrying a cardboard box. "Lorna gave me an apple pie, too," he explained rather sheepishly, as though a little embarrassed at Lorna's generosity.

Torey smiled, wanting to put Dex at ease. "I hope you enjoy it. As for working tomorrow, I really can't say. I'm sure it depends on how bad Rich's injury is. I'll call you later if Bart wants to work, okay?"

"Okay. I'll see you either tomorrow or Monday then."

"Fine."

Dex took a few steps, then stopped. "Torey, if you find out how Rich is, let me know about it."

"I will, Dex."

When Dex was gone, Torey walked around and picked up tools. There were three shovels, the axe and hammer the men had used to break down the boxes the trees had arrived in and the garden hose. When the tools were all in one spot beside the tractor, Torey turned on the hose and began spraying the newly planted trees.

Lorna came out from the house. "I'm worried about Rich."

"Did you see the cut?"

"Not really. Did you?"

Torey nodded. "It needs stitches, all right, but it's not that bad, Lorna. A head cut bleeds so much that it scares the tar out of everyone. Rich will be fine, I'm sure."

"Well, I suppose I might as well put some of that sauce in freezer containers. You and me couldn't eat it all if we had spaghetti every night for a week." Lorna's face brightened. "Say, I could bring some of it over to the Scanlons' for their dinner."

"Yes, but heaven only knows how long they'll be gone. Sometimes it takes hours to get treated in the Emergency Room."

Lorna frowned again. "That's true. Well, maybe I'll wait a little while before I freeze any of it. Did Bart say he'd let us know how Rich is?"

"No, but I'm hoping he will. I didn't think about it before he left, but I intend to pay for Rich's treatment. He wouldn't have been hurt if he hadn't been working here today."

Lorna nodded in agreement. "Those boys—Bart, too— kind of tug at your heartstrings, don't they? I have the feeling that they're all trying so hard."

Torey sighed softly. Apparently she wasn't the only one who'd seen another side of the Scanlon family today. "Yes," she said quietly. "They all three tug at your heartstrings."

"Torey?"

"Yes?"

"You're drowning that tree, honey."

Eleven

To Torey's surprise and Lorna's elation, the Scanlons drove up a little after five. Rich, with a bandage covering the left side of his forehead, was a trifle pale, but smiling. "I didn't want to miss that spaghetti dinner," he told Lorna, who promptly insisted the injured young man lie down on the living-room sofa. Briskly, Lorna smoothed a clean white sheet over the pale blue upholstery and directed a mildly protesting Rich to the makeshift bed. "I didn't mean to cause you more trouble," he told her.

Rob was grinning from ear to ear. Torey and Bart were standing by, all three watching Lorna mother-henning Rich. "I hope coming back for dinner is all right," Bart said in an undertone to Torey.

"Of course it is," she said quietly. "By the way, I plan to reimburse you for the Emergency Room charges. I'll write a check right now if you'll tell me the amount." She was surprised to see a strange look of withdrawal in Bart's eyes. "I insist, Bart," she quickly added.

He ignored the subject. "Would you mind if Rob and I washed up?"

Lorna intervened. "Heavens, no. Go right ahead. The bathroom's down that hall."

Bart's gaze flicked over Torey. He knew very well where the bathroom was, but Torey interpreted the look to be a reminder of *how* he knew.

It was a reminder she didn't need. Last Sunday afternoon was indelibly imprinted on her brain, every single second of it. But today's events were a strange influence. Her aggressiveness in the toolshed, followed by Rich's accident, then an almost startling understanding of the Scanlon family, were factors Torey wasn't able to ignore. Oddly, there seemed to have been a subtle shifting of roles with her and Bart, she realized, as if they were reversing their previous attitude on involvement. Now, he seemed to be forgetting his hard stand, while she was backing away.

It would always be that way, she suspected. Given Bart's immutable plans for his and the twins' future, he would constantly be running hot and cold with a woman. When the attraction was too strong to combat, he would soften toward her. When he was sexually satisfied, he would see again that more than one resolute, preoccupying commitment was impossible, and his first and foremost commitment was to his brothers.

In simpler terms, anything with Bart would be an affair, a sexually unrestrained and emotionally draining affair. Understanding Bart much better than she had, Torey knew she was afraid of it.

Lorna seemed to be in seventh heaven, humming while she dished up a bountiful dinner. An immense green salad, quarts of milk, toasted garlic bread and mountains of spaghetti smothered in rich sauce were gobbled up by the

Scanlons. Lorna beamed when the three men wanted seconds, and then she proudly served apple pie and ice cream for dessert. "There's a chocolate cake, too," she told them.

As they finished the last bites of dessert, Bart brought up the tree-planting project. "Rob and I will be over tomorrow morning to finish the job."

Torey raised her eyes. "I'll call Dex. I promised to let him know how Rich was doing anyway." She recalled having been told that the Scanlons always serviced their logging equipment on Sunday mornings. "If you have something else you need to do however..."

Bart shook his head. "No, we'll get this done first."

Rob leaned back with a satisfied sigh and patted his youthful, flat-as-a-board stomach. "That was the best food I've ever tasted. Thanks, Lorna." Rich seconded the compliment, and Torey could see that Lorna had been completely won over by those "scamps," the Scanlon twins.

"At least I can tell you two apart now," Torey teased. "Rich has a bandage on his forehead, Rob doesn't."

The boys laughed. "When we were kids, we even fooled Bart a few times," Rob said. "One time, when we were in the fifth grade, I had studied for a test and Rich hadn't. Rich pretended he was sick and I went and took the test. I passed with a good grade. The next day, Rich was supposed to take a makeup test, so we switched identities. I went to school as Rich and took the test again. He stayed home as me, pretending that I had caught his bug and was too sick to go to school."

Everyone laughed, but then Bart cocked an eyebrow at his brothers. "Tell them what happened after that."

Rob shook his head tragically. "Bart figured it out and made us go to the principal and tell him what we did. We both got detention for two weeks. No recesses."

"We could go on and on with such entertaining little stories," Bart said dryly. "These two haven't exactly been angels. But I think we better get Rich home. He looks a little droopy. Lorna, I'll help with the dishes first, then—''

"You most certainly will not! You get this boy home and put him to bed," Lorna exclaimed, obviously aghast that Bart would even suggest a delay.

Torey had been avoiding direct eye contact with Bart, but she knew she was going to have to tell him that tonight was off. She wasn't going to interfere in the Scanlon family's plans again. The twins *weren't* scamps or do-nothings and they deserved the chance to become physicians as much as anyone else. It was almost criminal that she had let old antagonisms prevent her from knowing the Scanlons better, but she wasn't going to compound the sin by intruding on their lives now.

Chairs were pushed back from the table and the Scanlons again expressed thanks and compliments for Lorna's good dinner. Torey noted Rob steadying his brother with a hand on Rich's arm as they walked through the house, and she suddenly had a choking sensation to deal with. The Scanlons' affection for each other was so natural, so real, that it affected her emotionally. And she sensed that it affected Lorna, too.

They were all outside on the front porch when Bart said calmly, "I'll see you at eight, Torey."

Everyone looked at her. Slightly off balance from their curiosity, Torey took a deep breath. Her gaze skittered to Bart. "Would you mind terribly if I begged off, Bart?" She saw instantly that he minded a lot. Or, at least, he minded the question being put to him in front of his brothers and Lorna. A nerve twitched in his jaw for a moment, and then his eyes grew cooler and he nodded.

"No problem. See you tomorrow."

It had been lousy timing. She should have found a way to tell him without an audience. Troubled, she watched the three Scanlons get into Bart's pickup and drive away.

Lorna seemed uneasy, too. "Did you and Bart have a date planned for tonight?"

Torey stopped chewing on her bottom lip. "We talked about it earlier, yes."

"But you changed your mind?"

The dust on the long driveway was settling, and Torey kept staring at it. "It seemed best after everything that happened."

"I don't think Bart liked it."

Torey sighed. "He didn't like talking about it in front of you and the twins. Let's go in and do the dishes."

The rest of the trees were planted by noon the next day. Dex, Rob and Bart worked without a break until the last one was in the ground. Torey had skipped church again, but Lorna went and returned and then invited the three men to stay for lunch. Dex looked ready to agree until Bart refused with thanks. "Rob and I have some other work to take care of yet today, Lorna."

When the black pickup sped away, Lorna frowned after it. "They work too hard, Torey. Those boys should at least have Sundays off. Bart, too, for that matter."

"I know," Torey quietly agreed. Bart had been as distant as the stars, which was what she had opted for, but it had created a piercing ache within her. Torey suspected that particular discomfort would stay with her for a long, long time.

The tree project was completed, though, and there would be little reason now and in the future for her and Bart to see much of each other. Like before, they would run into each other occasionally. The chance meetings would be even more painful than they used to be, but for an entirely different reason. Now, whenever she saw Bart, her own memory would play cruel tricks on her. All she could hope for was that, eventually, life would return to normal.

Lorna had changed from a going-to-church outfit to a cotton housedress, but Torey saw that her friend and companion seemed too distracted to adhere to usual Sunday afternoon routines. When Lorna didn't go visiting after church, she spent the day quietly, reading the newspaper, knitting, doing some light cooking, sometimes watching a little television. Today, she quickly flipped through the newspaper, paced the house at intervals and sighed often. After a while, Lorna's absentminded nervousness increased Torey's own restlessness.

She knew the Scanlons were in both of their minds, and she was almost relieved when Lorna began talking about them. "I just can't believe that I've lived so close to that family all these years and never concerned myself with their welfare," Lorna finally declared.

"I don't think Bart ever wanted anyone's concern, Lorna."

"No, he never asked anything of anyone, did he? But neighbors shouldn't have to ask, Torey. It's amazing, really, but I don't even think your grandparents were very aware of the Scanlons."

"Only because of Bart's stubborn independence. Granddad and Grandma helped anyone who needed it. For that matter, no one could be any more generous than you are, Lorna."

The older woman frowned. "Well, I haven't been very generous with Bart and the twins." Her expression softened. "They're good boys, Torey. High-spirited, yes. And I know they've gotten themselves into a few scrapes. But they're honest and hardworking. They've never been in trouble with the law, or with drugs. Everyone knows the young people in the area who break the important rules."

Torey smiled wryly. "Bart would probably have skinned them alive if they had ever fooled around with drugs."

"Exactly. Bart's the strength in that family. He's done an incredible job, Torey. Just think about it. He was only twenty years old when his father died. He gave up his own hopes and dreams to come home and care for his eight-year-old brothers. I'll tell you something, young lady. Bart Scanlon is okay in my book."

He was okay in her book, too, Torey acknowledged, noting that Lorna's opinion of Bart had been defensively stated, as if in expectation of opposition. Torey got a sense of where the conversation was going. "You want to help them out, don't you?"

"Would you mind?"

"Lorna, I would never presume to interfere with anything you might want to do. But what *could* you do? The twins are grown. It's not as though Bart needs a baby-sitter."

Lorna's eyes had taken on a warm sparkle. "For starters, our freezer is full of good food. I'd like to take that container of beef stew I froze last week over to them, and that chocolate cake I baked yesterday is just going to go to waste. It's barely been touched."

Wondering just where that sort of interaction might lead, Torey hesitated. She'd just been thinking that she and Bart wouldn't be seeing much of each other from here on in, which should ultimately ease the tension she was living with. Still, Lorna taking it upon herself to see that Rob and Rich Scanlon had a nourishing meal now and then didn't really involve her and Bart.

"Do whatever you want to, Lorna," she said quietly.

Lorna nodded happily. "I knew you'd feel that way. I think I'll run on over to the Scanlons' right now. Rich will be there, I'm sure."

Torey followed her to the kitchen, where Lorna busily began gathering up food. "By the way, Bart has three very unfriendly dogs, Lorna. Be careful."

"I've never been afraid of dogs," Lorna replied with complete confidence.

"I know, but those three could spook anyone. Just watch for them."

With a reflective frown, Torey watched Lorna driving away. Under other circumstances, she would have gone with Lorna. The older woman was always eager to help out where she could, and Torey often participated in Lorna's charitable acts. But inviting further friendship with the Scanlons could only end up bad. For the twins, for Bart and for herself, it was best that she stay completely away from them.

Feeling fidgety, Torey decided to take care of a job she'd filed away in the back of her mind as needing doing when she had the time. The tack room, located in the barn, was in need of a good cleaning, and armed with a pail of warm, soapy water and clean rags, Torey headed for the barn.

First she swept the room out with the barn broom, then she began wiping down shelves and work benches. Within an hour, the dust she'd been battling had been effectively transferred to herself. She was wearing shorts and a halter top, and her skin was beginning to feel gritty.

Hearing a car, Torey thought Lorna must have returned. She stepped outside the barn to let Lorna know where she was. A feeling very close to an electrical shock brought her up short. It wasn't Lorna's car stopping beside the house; it was Bart's black pickup!

He got out of the truck and started directly for her. Lamenting that he wouldn't have known where she was if she hadn't shown herself was wasted effort; Bart was bearing down on her with a walk that boded no good.

As he got closer, Torey could see he was still in work clothes, the same jeans and blue shirt he'd been wearing that morning. His expression was dark, stormy and impatient-looking, and he stopped in front of Torey with his hands on his hips. She wondered why he was so steamed up, but certainly didn't learn the reason from his harshly put, "It's up to you to put a stop to this."

Genuinely perplexed, Torey blinked. "Put a stop to what?"

Bart's expression only got harder. "Don't play games with me. You know damned well what Lorna's doing over at my place."

"Yes, I know what she's doing. She brought some stew and a chocolate cake over for the twins."

Bart's lip curled. "She's *cleaning!*"

"She's what?"

"You heard me. She's cleaning the house!"

Torey slumped back against the wall of the barn. She should have known if Lorna got one look at the Scanlons' disreputable house, she wouldn't be able to ignore it. Torey could just see her rolling up her sleeves and diving in. A dirty house was a challenge to Lorna, just as the possibility of an improper diet for growing boys was.

The imagined scene struck Torey as sort of comical, but laughing in Bart's tense face didn't seem overly bright. Battling an urge to giggle, and in defense of Lorna's zeal, Torey retorted, "Well, it *needs* cleaning, doesn't it?"

A prideful, stubborn light gleamed in Bart's eyes. "I'll do my own damned cleaning."

"Why didn't you tell her that? Why come over here and lay it on me?" Torey saw Bart uncomfortably shift his weight from one foot to the other, and a light bulb went on in her head. "You don't want to hurt her feelings, do you? In fact, you *can't* hurt her feelings."

The Bart Scanlon Torey was getting to know better all the time completely amazed her. She knew she shouldn't bring up even a hint of what had transpired between them, not if she wanted to maintain an impersonal distance. But she couldn't stop herself. "Tell me something, Bart. Why, when you're really nothing but a big softy inside, were you able to torment me for so many years? Didn't it ever bother you to make me cry?"

Bart looked away. "We were only kids then."

That wasn't entirely true, but Torey let it pass. "Which made it all right?"

"I told you I liked you. I guess I was just a dumb kid who didn't know how to show my feelings."

She almost said, "You're not a dumb kid now." But she didn't. Instead, she turned and went back into the barn and on into the tack room. Tossing the cleaning rag she'd been carrying into the pail of water, she glanced back at Bart, who'd followed and was leaning against the doorframe. "You'll have to tell Lorna yourself if you don't want her over there. I can't hurt her feelings, either."

Bart was studying Torey. She was beautiful and sexy and a continual itch. "Why did you back out last night?"

Torey took a breath before she answered. "Because I finally understood your priorities. I'm not going to be the person to come between you and the twins and your goal, Bart."

"What brought all that understanding on?"

"Seeing the three of you together. It's very obvious how close you are to one another."

Bart was bareheaded, and he suddenly raked his hair, a gesture conveying deep agitation. "I can't stop thinking about you. I can't stop thinking about last Sunday. I don't want you going out with Steve Johnson, or any other man."

Torey's heart had started an unmerciful hammering. "I won't be going out with Steve again. I broke that up. But you and I both have to realize that eventually—"

"No! Don't say it." Bart started across the room. "I don't know what to do about us, but I can't let you slip away." He reached Torey's space and put his hands on her shoulders. His eyes were dark blue and brooding. "If I wasn't dirty from working all day, I'd want . . ."

Torey's blood was racing, her insides suddenly hot and roiling. All the good sense in the world couldn't eliminate what Bart made her feel. His nearness, his touch, were drugging, muddying her noble intentions. She stared into his eyes. "I'm dirty, too," she whispered. "What do you want?"

With a groan, he pulled her forward. His mouth moved over her face. "I want to make love to you," he whispered. "I want to soak in your moisture, to feel again the way your body squeezes around mine. I want to kiss your breasts. I want you to kiss me, to touch me. I want to make love to you standing up, sitting down, in every position I ever even heard of."

"Oh, Bart," she moaned on a sob.

"Don't be shocked."

"I'm not shocked. I want the same things." There was so much love in Torey's soul, she thought she might burst from it. What had made her think she could just set it aside, pretend it wasn't an abiding part of her? Dare she talk about it? Dare she say, "I love you, Bart," and give them even more anguish?

Their mouths met in a gasping, needful kiss, and they tore at each other's clothing. Whatever came to them in the future, they had to have one another now. The clouds of passion parted briefly for Torey. "Upstairs . . . Granddad's workroom," she rasped. Taking Bart by the hand, she led him from the tack room and to the ladder leading to the barn's second story.

Hay hadn't been stored in the loft for years, but it still bore the aroma of alfalfa. Torey opened a door. "Granddad fixed this room up for his hobbies. He worked with leather and wood."

Bart followed her in. "A bed?"

"It's small. I remember Granddad napping up here sometimes."

"It's big enough. Come here."

Torey walked into his arms. She could feel the throb of his desire. "This is crazy," she whispered in a moment of clarity. "We shouldn't be doing this."

"I can't stop myself." His hands were hot on her skin. The halter top was easily disposed of, and his eyes ignited to burning coals at the sight of her bare breasts. "You're beautiful, Torey, the most beautiful woman I've ever seen."

She was unbuttoning his shirt. "And pretty, too?" she teased.

"Pretty and beautiful and smart and sexy."

"Not so smart," she rebutted softly, then parted his shirt and pressed her lips to his chest. "Oh, Bart," she whispered. "I'm so confused about us."

"About this?"

"No, not about this. I don't seem to have any control over wanting you. But the rest of it . . . ?"

His mouth came down. "Don't talk. Not now. We'll talk later."

They finished undressing, driven to haste by need of one another. Kisses were brief and hot, caresses were demanding and wildly arousing. They moved to the small bed. Torey laid down first and Bart covered her with his body. Neither wanted any foreplay, neither needed it. Cradled within the heat of Torey's opened thighs, Bart surged into her. "Oh, honey," he whispered raggedly.

The poor little bed creaked in protest from its double, rocking load, but if it would have collapsed and thrown its occupants onto the floor, neither would have cared. Torey's legs wrapped around Bart's hips, and his plunges went deeper and deeper, reaching that part of her that was in flames and shrieking for release.

It came quickly, in a rush of tears and mind-shattering pleasure. She held on tight as he prolonged the ecstatic spasms with a harder, faster tempo. Then his cry—"Torey!"—filled the room, and he fell on her in a trembling heap. Their labored breathing gradually subsided.

Torey's eyes were closed. The first moments after intensely satisfying lovemaking, she had learned just last Sunday, were unique and extremely special. The man weighting her down, holding her to the ancient little bed, was at peace, as she was. It couldn't possibly last, she knew, but she clung to the feeling, as strongly as she was clinging to Bart.

He raised his head. His gaze moved over her face. "Do you ever think about love?"

Her eyes became large and alert. "Yes, of course. Do you?"

"I'm thinking about it now. Are we falling in love with each other, Torey?"

He didn't look particularly happy about it, she saw. This wildness between them was disrupting everything he'd been working so hard for. "And if we were?" she whispered.

He shook his head slowly. "I don't know. I just don't know."

She saw him dampen his lips, and then he placed them on hers. The kiss had a rather helpless quality to it at first, but it rapidly evolved into desire. "I want you again," he whispered. "Maybe I'll never get enough of you."

They made love slowly, provocatively, for a very long time. Bart was a tireless lover, Torey discovered. He was a strong man with hard muscles and callused hands, and it tore at her heartstrings that those same hands would have been administering to the sick without the cruel twist of fate that had destroyed Bart's dreams.

Their personal relationship, so long a tribulation she had done her best to avoid, seemed utterly ludicrous and a terrible waste of precious time to her now. Why hadn't she been able to see through Bart's taunts to the boy, the young man, the adult, he'd really been?

Again, vows and fears and emotions were rearranging within her. Her ambivalence was maddening, but also proved that she wasn't so rigid that she couldn't adjust. Maybe she *could* live with a meaningful affair. There wasn't much room in her mind for doubts about her and Bart seeking each other out every chance they got; that was becoming more incontrovertible with each passing day. And he was thinking about love, the same as she was. If they were both a little cautious about bringing it out into the open, that was understandable, too.

Still, where could it all go? It was a painfully frustrating situation.

After they had dressed and returned to the first floor of the barn, Bart held her for a long, lovely moment. "I wonder if we could meet here without Lorna catching on," he mused softly.

"I think she might wonder why I'm dashing out to the barn after dark, don't you?" Torey returned with a note of humor.

Bart laughed quietly. "Yes, I expect she would. I wonder if she's through cleaning yet."

"She's not home, so apparently not."

With their arms around each other's waists, they began walking to Bart's pickup. "I didn't know what to say when Rob and I got home and Lorna was up to her elbows in scrub water."

"Just tell her thanks, Bart. Lorna's a good person. Whatever she's doing for the Scanlons, it's with only the best of intentions."

"I'm sure of that, but my house was so damned dirty, Torey. The boys and I give it a lick and a promise every so often, but we just don't have the time to keep it up. It's not so bad during the winter months, but while we're logging, there's rarely a spare hour."

"Yet you came over here and put in those trees." Torey frowned at the tidy row of poplars. "I owe you an apology."

Bart stopped walking and looked down at her. "Because of the trees?"

"Because of my attitude on the road. I'm beginning to think it was nothing but petty vindictiveness."

He smiled. "Well, maybe I owe you an apology, too. You wouldn't have been looking for revenge if I hadn't made your childhood miserable. You were just so darned cute I couldn't leave you alone." He gave her a kiss, one that started out light and playful. But then he turned and hugged her close and kissed her deeply. His eyes were smoky when he looked at her "I could make love to you again right this minute."

Shaken, Torey touched his mouth. Their feelings were multiplying by leaps and bounds. This was getting very, very serious. "I could make love to you again, too," she said softly. "But Lorna could be returning at any minute."

He nibbled at her fingers. "We'll have to be patient, I guess."

Torey was in the house when Lorna came bursting in an hour later. The older woman was breathless with excitement. "You'll never guess what I've been doing!"

There was a smudge on Lorna's cheek and her pale yellow cotton housedress was soiled and wrinkled. "Changing a tire?" Torey teased.

"Cleaning the Scanlon house! Torey, you have never seen such a mess in your entire life. There were twenty pairs of dirty jeans in the laundry room. *Twenty!* And the underwear and the shirts? Why, I couldn't believe my own eyes.

The kitchen sink was overflowing with dirty dishes, and the rest of the house was beyond description. Well, just let me say that it looks a lot different now.''

Lorna went to the refrigerator for some iced tea. ''How's Rich feeling?'' Torey asked.

''He had a terrible headache when I got there, which is to be expected after a knock on the head. I gave him some aspirin and made him go to bed. Not until I put clean sheets on it, though.'' After a swallow of tea, Lorna's face brightened. ''Torey, the Scanlon house is really nice. Once you can see it,'' she added wryly.

''I've been there, Lorna.''

''Well, it's twice as big as this one. Do you know that it has five bedrooms and two really large bathrooms?''

''With three sons, I suppose they needed a large house.''

''I expect so. Anyway, it could be a splendid home with a woman's touch.''

''Oh?''

''Oh, it needs a thorough going-over, don't get me wrong. The carpets are dreadful things, and the whole place needs new paint and wallpaper. But it has marvelous oak cabinetry and woodwork.'' Lorna gave Torey a rather intense look. ''You know, the twins will be gone for most of the next eight, ten years, and then who knows where they'll be after that? Bart will be rattling around in that big place all by himself.''

Torey sat down at the kitchen table, absorbing the innuendo in Lorna's comment. Other than money, was there any real reason for Bart to avoid a personal relationship? Come September, the twins would begin their long siege of education. They would be home for holidays and the summer months, but Bart's perpetual attention was drawing to a close. Did he really understand that?

My Lord, was she thinking of marriage? Yes, educating two ambitious young men was going to be costly, but was there anything wrong with a wife helping her husband out financially? Not that Torey was loaded with money, but she had a nice bank account and the ranch consistently showed a respectable profit.

Where there was true love, there was always a way, Torey thought with mounting excitement. After today, true love didn't seem at all out of reach. Her biggest job, though, and maybe the most crucial of her life, was going to be convincing the proudly independent Mr. Bart Scanlon that pooling their assets made good sense.

Twelve

"**A**bsolutely not! Why would you think I'd even consider taking money from you?"

They were sitting on the patio, and Torey had approached the subject of money very cautiously. Not cautiously enough, apparently, because Bart's face had turned cold and forbidding.

She returned the hard look in his eyes. "Not even if it meant that you and I...?" Torey stopped as humiliation surged through her. She couldn't believe her own temerity. Why, she was practically asking Bart to marry her! Which, she found out in the next breath, he understood very well.

"Even if you and I got married tonight I wouldn't touch your money," he said with disdainful distinction. "What the hell kind of man do you think I am?"

Her face was burning. They were talking about marriage only because she had forced the issue. The indignity she felt had been self-induced, but Bart's inflexibility still galled. "One with a very outdated philosophy," she retorted sharply. Rising, Torey went to the edge of the patio, folded her arms across her chest and stared out into the dark. "I should have known you'd have chauvinistic viewpoints," she muttered.

Bart got up and came up behind her. "Because I won't take a woman's money, I'm a chauvinist?" he said, disgust in his voice.

Torey turned around. "What if it was the other way around? What if I needed money?"

"That's different."

"Oh, give me strength," Torey groaned. "There's not a speck of difference in it except in your mind. You're a stubborn, stiff-necked—" Torey fumbled for the right word, and found none better than "—*man!*" Bart's responsive grin only made her feel like smacking him one.

"Do you want me to apologize for being a man?" he drawled suggestively. "We wouldn't have near as much fun together if I weren't, honey."

"Please don't start teasing me. I don't find this at all amusing."

Bart couldn't believe that Torey had actually offered him money. It was such a ludicrous notion, he had already put it out of his mind. Laughing softly because she looked so damned cute all worked up, he dropped his arms around her, with his thoughts in an entirely different vein. "Let's take a walk," he whispered, eyeing the black shadow of the barn in the distance. "Lorna's watching TV. She'll never miss us."

The request birthed a wave of tempting images: an arm-in-arm walk to the barn and to the second-story hobby room with its rickety little bed. Torey's insides began heating up. Whatever else caused discord in their lives, there was no doubting the chemistry between them.

But no, Bart had been tired when he'd arrived and they'd decided to sit on the patio and talk. Torey had seen it as a golden opportunity to broach a plan that made more sense every time she thought about it. If Bart was losing his fatigue at the prospect of making love, he could just go take a cold shower, she decided spitefully, denying herself to prove a point.

Bart didn't wait for an answer, though. He started kissing her, creating vibrant, persuasive little meetings between his lips and her temples, the corners of her mouth, an earlobe. The thrills of potent sexuality rippled through Torey, clouding the objections she'd been lining up. Her eyelashes drifted downward while her hands slid up his chest. The hard muscles beneath her fingers ignited her imagination, while Bart's delightfully unhurried rain of kisses battered her defenses.

The evening was warm, and because Torey had wanted to look her best when she presented her monetary proposal—knowing instinctively that Bart wasn't going to just jump at the idea, and that she had better use every advantage she might have to sway his hardheaded pridefulness—she had dressed in the lovely buttery-colored sundress she'd been saving for a special occasion. Torey knew Bart liked the dress. He'd mentioned it when he'd first arrived and the warm admiration in his eyes had kept her confident of her appearance.

Until she had started talking about money. Even then, while she felt Bart withdrawing, Torey had seen his gaze lingering on her bare shoulders and throat and the upper swells of her breasts at the top of the dress.

Now, he seemed intent on exploring the fine, silky-soft fabric. His big, callused hands drifted as arousingly on her body as his mouth was doing on her face. Torey's breathing pattern was changing, her partially opened mouth taking in quick, gasping little puffs of air.

"We're...not through talking," she whispered raggedly, which was a rather fruitless protest against making love on the patio when she was responding to his every caress.

"Oh, yes we are." Bart's mouth covered hers and settled into a real kiss. His hands moved down her back to her bottom and brought her closer. Locked together, the hardness in his jeans burned into Torey's abdomen. He slowly and heatedly rubbed against her while his tongue searched her mouth.

"Let's go to the barn," he whispered, hot and urgently. "I love this dress, but I want you out of it. I want to peel down your panties and open your thighs. I want to kiss you and taste you."

Torey's heart skipped several beats. The picture Bart had incited was erotically stimulating. She could easily see what he wanted to do, and her body ached with a staggering burst of desire.

But she already knew all about Bart's sexual power. What she didn't know was how they were going to reconcile their differences. Especially when he discarded possible avenues of action without even discussing them because of too much stubborn pride.

Her voice was low and husky with emotion. "You're an impossible man. I've come up with a perfectly logical solution to our problem, and..." She felt Bart let go of her very abruptly and teetered for a moment.

"Not *our* problem, Torey. *My* problem. And it already has a solution. I have enough timber on that mountain to pay for the boys' education. Fortunately, it's a year-by-year expenditure." The passion on Bart's face had deteriorated to a scowl. "I'll cover it just fine, and I don't want you worrying about it."

Torey stiffened. He was shutting her out, excluding her from the situation. Maybe that hurt even more than his stubborn machismo. A spark of retaliatory anger hardened Torey's voice. "I'm not worrying about that, but you're using it as an excuse to..."

"To stay single?"

There was a gibing sarcasm in Bart's tone, which caused Torey to wilt again from her own boldness. Bart had never said "I love you" to her. Asking if she ever thought about love was as close to the subject as he'd gotten, and here she was, just inviting ridicule. Where was *her* pride? Bart wore his like a banner, but where in hell had hers disappeared to?

Why had she fallen for this particular man? Why, after years of animosity, was Bart Scanlon the man she wanted to be with, live with, love and laugh and cry with?

The answer struck Torey with startling clarity. With Bart she knew exactly who and what she was. It was Bart who defined the female in her. It was Bart who made her recognize and accept her own sexuality. With Bart she was whole, a complete woman. She had never experienced that feeling with any other man.

It was maddeningly frustrating to see things so clearly when he refused to, and infuriating to realize there was nothing she could do to change his mind.

Bart spoke quietly then, without sarcasm, without anger. "I won't ask any woman to comply with my goals. Especially you, Torey. You deserve so much more."

Torey's mouth dropped open. His reasoning left her cold. "Like meeting you in the barn when you need a woman?"

Bart became very still. "Is that what you really think?" His eyes narrowed on her face for a few tense moments, then he took her arm in a none too gentle hold. "Chew on this, Torey. Sex is not a scarce commodity. I don't have to come around here when I need a woman. We both know we've got something special, and I don't like sneaking around any more than you do. But right now, there's nothing else I can do."

Her eyes flashed angrily. Arguing was futile, and she knew that, but she couldn't force herself to shut up. "You won't even consider anything else."

"I won't consider taking money from you, that's for damned sure!" Bart let go of her arm. "I'm going home. There's no point to this argument." He walked off of the patio, heading in the direction of the driveway.

Torey watched him rebelliously, deluged by a dozen different and yet undeniably connected impulses. She felt boxed in, trapped by Bart's narrow-minded, completely illogical attitude. At the last second, just before he reached his pickup, she yelled, "Will you at least think about it?"

Bart's reply lashed the night air. "No! Forget it, Torey. Just drop it!"

When the sound of Bart's pickup had died out, Torey angrily plopped into a chair. A few minutes of hopeless frustration passed before she realized she was crying. Tears were trickling down her cheeks. It took another few minutes of sniffling and wiping the damp trails away before she faced a painful, soul-searing fact: Bart Scanlon had made her cry again.

It renewed her fury. Whether she hated or loved the arrogant jerk, he retained the ability to make her cry!

No more. God in heaven, no more!

With Bart's brick-wall, sexist attitude, she could never expect more from him than she had right now, an occasional meeting to make love. She would have to be demented to sentence herself to years of this kind of pain.

Rising, she went into the house. After finding a tissue and blowing her nose, she joined Lorna in the living room. The older woman took one look at her red eyes and switched off the television set. "Did you and Bart have words again?"

"Oh, we had words, all right," Torey said bitterly, perching on the edge of a sofa cushion. "He's the most pigheaded know-it-all in the entire state."

Lorna was silent a moment, then heaved a sigh. "But you're in love with him."

Torey sat quite still while her gaze tangled with Lorna's. "Apparently I haven't done a very good job of keeping my feelings to myself," she said slowly.

"I know you very well, Torey." Lorna hesitated. "I know this is no one's business but your own, but I'm concerned about you. Are you and Bart...lovers?"

Lorna had stumbled over the word. Torey knew Lorna's disapproving views on the relaxed mores of modern relationships, and knew, too, that even mentioning the subject was costly to the older woman. Only a deeply-rooted concern for Torey's welfare would have prompted the question.

There was no longer a reason for pretense, and Torey leaned back against the sofa with a long, rueful sigh. "I've been a fool, I guess."

"Women are often foolish when they fall in love," Lorna said softly. "Does Bart return your feelings?"

"I don't honestly know," Torey replied wearily. "Sometimes I think yes, very definitely, yes, and then I have to wonder. He's completely wrapped up in the twins' future. Nothing else seems very important to him."

"I see. Is that what you argued about tonight?"

"More or less." Torey sat up straighter. "Lorna, do you see anything wrong with a woman financially helping the man she loves?"

"Did you propose that idea to Bart?"

"Yes, and he came unglued. He refused to even think about it."

"Well, that doesn't surprise me. Bart's a proud man." Lorna looked thoughtful for a moment. "I think he appreciated what I did in his house yesterday, though. I really only got started, however. I plan to go there again tomorrow."

Torey was taken aback. "You're not serious."

"Don't you think I should?"

"Uh...Lorna..." It was on the tip of Torey's tongue to tell Lorna that Bart hadn't been exactly thrilled about her generosity, but she just couldn't do it. "You should if you want to," she said instead, and got to her feet. "I'm going to go to bed. I've got some heavy thinking to do."

"About Bart."

"Yes, about Bart."

Lorna stood up. "Torey, I'm certainly no expert on the subject. I was in love only one time in my life, with my husband. We had only two short years together before he was killed in a car accident. That's when I came to the ranch. Your grandmother had a broken hip from a fall and needed help with the house. I arrived as a paid employee, but I stayed on as a friend and because your grandparents made me a part of the family." Lorna gave a brief laugh. "I've strayed from my point. What I wanted to say is that some women—maybe some men, too—only fall in love once. If you're really in love with Bart, try to understand his pride and determination."

"I have been trying," Torey said quietly. "But love is a two-way street, Lorna. He has to yield a little, too."

Torey brought that thought to bed with her. If Bart wouldn't yield even a tiny bit, they didn't stand much of a chance. Oh, they might go on for a long time with the present arrangement; there was too much going on between them to suppose their feelings might die out tomorrow.

The key word was feelings, wasn't it? Bart admitted there was something very special between them, and he'd also talked about love. He'd made it very clear that if all he wanted was physical release with a woman, he didn't have to hang around Torey Lancaster. One and one still made two, and unless she was only grasping at straws to appease the ache in her heart, Torey concluded that Bart was as much in love with her as she was with him.

Only, he was willing to live with an occasional evening or Sunday afternoon together and she wasn't. She wanted the whole nine yards, marriage, children, the works, and she was never going to see those lovely dreams reach fruition if she didn't do something.

Or *stop* doing something.

Did she have the strength of will to deny Bart—and herself—if he gave her one of those outlaw grins and started making love to her? His merest touch turned her legs to jelly. It would take a superhuman effort to halt the progression of their sexual relationship. Bart knew things about her now, which spots of her body to tease and caress, what kind of kisses made her moan for more.

Closing her eyes, Torey let the erotic image of Bart, naked and aroused, fill her mind. Her thoughts centered on what it was that she would be denying herself. If Bart turned to another woman, Torey knew that she might never get over it. But if abstinence made him realize just how much he did love her...?

Torey's eyelids jerked open. Was this too calculating? Too cold-blooded? Were any and all means to a happy ending really fair?

As it turned out, Torey had four days to search her conscience on the matter. It was Friday evening before she saw Bart again.

In the meantime, she received a bill for the poplars, which she promptly paid by putting a check for the full amount in the mail. She had made up her mind on one thing: Bart hadn't let her pay for Rich's Emergency Room treatment, and she wasn't going to accept anything from him for the trees.

It was a little after eight when Torey saw Bart's pickup on her driveway. Casting formality aside, she went out to meet him. The air was still warm from the hot day, but becoming silvery with long shadows. Bart climbed out of the truck with a smile and a "Hi."

Torey instantly realized Bart had put their last evening together completely out of his mind. Despite a tenacious thread of resentment, she decided to try and do the same. Picking up that argument would only result in another impasse, and Bart stalking off again would accomplish nothing.

"Hi," she returned with a soft smile.

He touched her hair, and a tingling thrill prickled Torey's spine. "You look beautiful," he said, gazing down at her with so much warmth, Torey's hopes leaped to life again.

She was wearing yellow slacks and a matching blouse, nothing special, she felt. But Bart's admiration made her feel beautiful. They *had* to work things out, they just had to. Maybe Bart didn't quite recognize—or simply couldn't allow himself to label—their feelings as love, but she had neither problem. Not anymore. "Thank you."

They continued to stare into each other's eyes. "Is Lorna home?"

Torey nodded silently.

"Let's go for a ride, then."

His intention, his desire for her, was on his face, in the depths of his riveting blue eyes. A private battle began in Torey. She wanted desperately to go with him, to do anything and everything he might ask. But she knew if she was going to go through with her plan, she had to start now. If she got in Bart's pickup and drove away with him, allowed him to find a place to make love, nothing would change.

When it was over, when he brought her back home, they would still be in the same quandary they were in right now.

It was decision time.

Torey took a deep breath. "Let's just sit on the patio," she said quietly, and saw a flicker of something unreadable on Bart's face.

"We sat on the patio Monday evening. Are you sure that's all you want to do tonight?"

No, that's not all I want to do! What I want is to lie in your arms, to take your kisses and your body, to have you, to hold you! Closing off that part of her brain and taking his arm, Torey urged him away from the pickup. "It's a beautiful night. Let's just sit under the stars and talk."

A frown appeared on Bart's face. "Maybe you'd like to go somewhere for a drink or a cup of coffee," he suggested hopefully.

"Lottie's?"

"No, not Lottie's."

They sat down. "Why not Lottie's, Bart? That first night we went out, why did you change your mind about taking me to Lottie's?"

"Because it's a dive."

"No, it's not," she said, mildly reproving. "Why would you think that?"

"You're full of questions tonight." He stared off broodingly. "I'm sorry I didn't get back over here until tonight. Are you upset about that?"

"I'm not upset about anything. Do I seem upset?"

"You seem..." Bart turned in his chair to see her better. "Why don't you want to go somewhere where we can be alone?"

"You're full of questions, too."

"Answer me, Torey."

She had another decision to make, Torey realized, whether or not to tell Bart right out what she was doing.

Which was best, to give him fair warning or to let him gradually figure it out?

No, she might be a bit calculating, but she wasn't deceitful. "All right," she said calmly. "I've come to a decision about us."

"And?" Bart prompted suspiciously.

"I completely understand and support your goal for the twins."

"*Their* goal, Torey."

"Yes, their goal. At any rate, I want you to know that I think what you're doing is admirable, very commendable."

"Thanks," he said dryly. "What about that decision you made? I have a feeling I'm not going to like it."

Torey laughed nervously. "Probably not."

Bart stared at her. "You're breaking this up, aren't you?"

She dropped her eyes. "You're very . . . perceptive."

"I'm not stupid."

"No, you're anything *but* stupid."

"All right," Bart sighed. "Why? Or, maybe I should ask, why now? When I made the same decision, you cornered me in the toolshed." He reached over and took her hand. "It's not going to work, you know. We need and want one another. Either I'll be over here after you or you'll come to my place."

Torey swallowed a lump in her throat that felt very much like unshed tears. This seemed so heartless, and wasn't what she wanted to do at all. But she couldn't just let things go on and on. If only Bart would just discuss options, or even let her know that he was willing to *look* for a solution. He was too complacently accepting of the situation, maybe too enmeshed in his longtime routines to see the forest for the trees.

She knew that she had to be scrupulously honest right now, no matter how Bart took it. "No, I won't," she said evenly. "I want you to face your feelings, Bart."

He raised an eyebrow and a strained silence ensued. When he finally replied, it was with defensiveness. "I think I've faced my feelings."

Torey gathered up her courage. "All right, fine. But if you have, you've kept them pretty much to yourself. Let me ask you a question. Do you love me?"

Bart's eyes narrowed into accusing slits. "You don't beat around the bush, do you?"

"That was a simple, straightforward question, Bart. Can you answer it?" Torey's heart was thumping so hard, she could hear it in her own ears.

The evening air was suddenly thick enough to cut with a knife. Bart's stare wasn't very complimentary, and Torey had to fight an urge to squirm beneath it. She saw the flickering of emotion in his eyes and prayed that he would let it out. Even genuine anger at this point could be a positive step. At least then they might get to some very basic truths. What she couldn't bear was Bart's attitude that she wasn't involved in the part of his life that encompassed his responsibilities to his brothers.

She saw his lip curl and felt a dead weight in her stomach. At the same time a certainty developed that he was going to remain adamantly stubborn. "Yes, I can answer it, but I'm not going to." He dropped her hand back into her lap and stood up. "Women just can't resist pushing a man, can they?"

Moving around in front of Torey, Bart bent over and put his hands on the arms of her chair. His face stopped only an inch from hers. "You'll give in before I will, sweetheart," he said low and positively. "Like I told you before, when you want me, you know right where to find me."

Smiling then, he rumpled her hair. Torey drew her head back, stung that he would purposely regress to that sort of innuendo after all that had occurred between them. He apparently didn't believe she was serious and thought he could kid her out of it. He was also annoyingly sure of himself. "You think this is only a game, don't you?" Torey said hoarsely, her throat so tight it was painful to speak.

He laughed softly. "What I think is that you're a conniving female, sweetheart. But you're the sexiest conniving female in three states. See you around."

Bart strolled off, and Torey cursed his strutting peacock walk. Every conceited line of his body made her twitch with fury. She would give in before him? Not on a bet! Not for all the tea in China! Not for—

Torey's mental tirade died an abrupt death. Already she wanted only to run after him, throw herself in his arms and plead temporary insanity. As the pickup drove off, Torey covered her face with her hands and groaned out loud. What had she gained, other than more anguish for herself?

Her ears picked up the sound of Bart's pickup coming back. Torey quickly dropped her hands and got to her feet. Maybe he had already seen her side of this fiasco, she thought with a rebirth of hope.

Bart left the motor running and got out. He walked back to her and held a small piece of blue paper out to her. "I forgot this."

Blindly, Torey took the paper. She looked down and saw that it was a check for five hundred and fifty dollars, half the cost of the poplars. "No, I don't want this," she protested.

Bart shrugged. "You've got it, want it or not."

Torey followed him to his pickup. "Bart, I'm not taking this money. You paid for Rich's treatment, and that's enough."

He gave her a salute that she saw as mocking, a brief gesture of forefinger to forehead. "So long, honey."

It wasn't until the pickup was gone that Torey realized she could have torn the check up in Bart's smug face. It wasn't half so satisfying to do it all by herself, but slowly and deliberately, she ripped the paper in two, and then again.

Thirteen

The rest of the summer passed much too slowly. Unbelievable as it seemed to Torey, Bart never called or came over even once. At first she was keyed up, in a state of waiting, relatively certain that he would just show up some evening. After a while, though, it became pretty clear that Bart's stubborn streak went even deeper than she'd thought.

Lorna and the twins seemed to have struck up a solid friendship, and through the older woman Torey was kept abreast of what was happening with the Scanlons. Torey suspected the basis of Lorna's and the twins' unlikely liaison was her cooking and their voracious appetites, but she never said so. Lorna thoroughly enjoyed the association, and was always eager to talk about it after a few hours or a day over at the Scanlons' house.

"Those boys will eat anything," she declared proudly.

"Anything that doesn't eat them first, I believe Bart said," Torey reminded dryly.

Lorna laughed. "You know how finicky and picky some young people are? Well, Rob and Rich just love vegetables. I prepare a grocery list every week, and one of them or Bart always manages to get to the market to buy the items. They do so love a good meal." Lorna sighed soulfully. "I'm sure going to miss those boys when they go off to college."

"So is Bart." Torey realized that she'd just mentioned Bart twice when ordinarily she avoided referring to him at all. Other than a distant glimpse, she'd seen nothing of Bart since the night he'd given her the check she had torn up, and it hurt horribly to even say his name.

"Oh, honey," Lorna said sadly. "Why don't you call him?"

Torey tensed. She couldn't be the one to give in, not on this. Not unless she was ready to fall into another loveless affair with Bart. Despite a terrible summer, Torey felt that she'd made the right decision. Her reply was a positive, "No, absolutely not."

"Pride is a cold companion, Torey."

"I'm sure Bart isn't spending every evening with only his pride."

"I wasn't talking about Bart, honey."

That little conversation gave Torey food for thought. She'd held out against hundreds of impulses to forget the stand she'd taken, and maybe if she really believed that Bart was battling the same impulses, she would have been less rigid. But she just didn't know what Bart was doing, other than working from sunup to sundown. Lorna relayed that information weekly, along with continuing laments that the dedicated threesome was working too hard, but even Lorna rarely saw Bart. There were a lot of visits to the Scanlons' house, Torey knew, where the older woman didn't even see the twins.

Torey never questioned Lorna's good deeds. One thing Torey knew with certainty was that Lorna's largesse was prompted by a genuine affection for the twins and a sincere regret that she hadn't been a better neighbor in the past.

The day finally came for the twins' departure. Lorna hinted at a farewell dinner, but Torey didn't relish the prospect of a forced get-together with Bart. He, obviously, had no trouble staying away from her, and it was almost as bad as a kick in the teeth to think of that, which she did much too often. Torey's entire summer was littered with spells of despondency, and she wondered if she could ever forgive Bart for his cavalier behavior, even if she was suddenly given the opportunity.

The party was ultimately held at the Scanlons' house and Torey sent over two packages, nicely gift-wrapped leather toiletry cases with appropriate, going-off-to-college cards.

Two weeks after that it began raining.

After weeks and weeks of unusual heat, Torey welcomed the cool, wet weather. She gave Dex a few days off and used the quiet, rainy days to catch up on her bookwork. With the twins gone, Lorna was sticking much closer to home, and it was she who answered the phone most of the time.

Torey was at her desk one afternoon when Lorna stuck her head in the room. "You have a call, Torey."

"Who is it?"

"Bart."

Torey's heart went *varoom* in her chest, and she sat back in her chair, instantly swamped with speculation. There were possible reasons for Bart to call; they were still neighbors, after all. Instinct or intuition or something she couldn't name told her this was a personal call, however.

"Are you going to take it?" Lorna asked rather anxiously.

It was hard to breathe. Torey felt almost choked. After nearly two months, Bart was calling. Why?

"Torey?"

"Yes, I'll take it." Torey's hand was shaking as she laid down the pen and reached for the phone. She cleared her throat. "Hello?"

"Hello, Torey. How are you?"

Just the sound of his voice told Torey that two months hadn't diminished her reactions to Bart Scanlon. Her mouth went instantly dry and her heart began beating overfast. She dampened her lips and took a quick breath. "I'm all right. How are you?" Torey heard a click as Lorna hung up the kitchen extension.

"All right, too, I guess."

A disconcerting silence brought a frown to Torey's face. She was about to say the first thing she might think of to break it when Bart asked, "Did the logging trucks give you much trouble this summer?"

"The trucks? Oh. No, not really."

"No dust?"

"Well, there was some dust, yes."

"Noise?"

It was almost as if Bart wanted her to complain about the trucks that had used the new road all summer. On the other hand, he didn't sound all that sure of himself, Torey realized, certainly not as cockily confident as she remembered. "The trees helped," she said, settling back in the chair, a little less tense than she'd been.

"I'd like to see you."

Torey closed her eyes. *That's* why he'd called, not to discuss how much dust or noise his trucks had created for two months. How many times had she envisioned a call like this? Was he merely hoping for a few hours together? What if he advanced and then backed off again? Could she take that? The summer had been far from easy, a nightmare of soul-searching, really. Sometimes she had cursed Bart, at other times she'd wept. At no time had she been without an ache in her heart.

She cleared her throat again. "Do... you want to come over here?"

"I think it would be better if you came over here. I'd like to talk to you in private."

She wasn't going to seek Bart's reason on the phone, nor did she intend to be coy. But it still took monumental effort to squelch the tide of questions beating in her brain. Torey's voice wasn't quite steady as she asked only one. "When do you want me to come?"

"Are you busy now?"

Giving the books and papers scattered across the desk a negligent glance, Torey said quietly, "I'm not doing anything that can't be put off. I'll drive over now." She heard Bart's relieved breath.

"Thanks, Torey."

"You're welcome. See you soon." Torey had no more than hung up when Lorna peeked around the door again.

"Dare I ask?" the older woman said hopefully.

Torey rose slowly. "He wants to talk to me. At his place. I told him I'd drive over."

Lorna seemed to relax all over, and her smile contained just a hint of smugness. "Well, now, isn't this something!"

Torey walked around the desk. "It could be about anything, Lorna. Don't let your imagination get carried away," she cautioned, even though her own pulse was running wild.

While she hurriedly changed clothes and brushed her hair, she was half afraid to really wonder why Bart wanted to talk to her. Surely her plan wasn't working at this late date. She'd all but given up on him ever understanding why she'd nipped their affair in the bud. For some time now, she'd been trying to convince herself to forget Bart, to view the brief romance as only an adult interlude. She had learned a lot about herself during those few weeks, and there really was nothing wrong with two mature people making love and then each going their separate ways.

Torey didn't get very far with that argument. She hadn't just made love with Bart, she'd fallen in love with him. Love was the core of her unhappiness, and she strongly suspected the episode with Bart would haunt her for the rest of her days.

During the short drive to the Scanlon place, it occurred to Torey, even through her nervous anticipation, that it had been raining the last time she'd gone over there, too. In fact, other than it being on the other end of summer, that day had been very much like this one, drizzling rain, gray, a little chilly.

When she pulled up beside the Scanlon house, Bart's three dogs came charging out of the barn, barking and carrying on as though they were bent on chewing up Torey's pickup. "How did Lorna get past you three brutes all summer?" Torey muttered. She blew the horn.

The front door opened and Bart came out. With only one word from him, the dogs settled down. Torey watched Bart walk out to the pickup. He looked wonderful, tall, slender and handsome in jeans and a white shirt. Her heart leaped around in her chest like a crazy thing. She was overjoyed to see him, even while she was leery of what might be coming. If all he wanted was to renew their affair, she suddenly became afraid that she might say yes and to hell with the rest of it. Seeing him made a world of difference, she realized uneasily.

Bart opened her door. "Hi."

Their gazes met and held. "Hi," she replied, striving for normalcy.

A slow smile spread over his face. "Come on in. Rain's dripping into my shirt collar."

A sense of déjà vu flitted through Torey's mind. "Watch that Sweetpea doesn't decide to have me for dinner," she said softly, reminding Bart of that other visit she'd made here.

He studied her, then understanding crept into his eyes. "We've got a lot to talk about." He held out his hand.

The tone of his voice made Torey's heart beat faster, his big, hard hand closing around hers increasing the sensation.

They crossed the yard and went into the house. Torey stared. The foyer was as neat as a pin. The wall pegs contained two jackets, one denim, one leather, and two hats. There wasn't even a speck of mud on the floor.

Bart brought her to the living room. It was neat and clean, too. Torey smiled reflectively, remembering the stocking that had decorated the arm of that one chair on her last visit. "Sit down," Bart invited. "Can I get you anything, a cup of coffee, maybe?"

"Nothing, thank you." Seated, Torey saw the big yellow cat lazily slinking into the room. It rubbed against her legs, then jumped onto her lap. Torey laughed softly. "Corky's a real friendly cat."

Bart sat on the couch. "Smart, too. He'd choose your lap over a goose-down pillow any day of the week."

Torey raised her eyes and looked across the room directly into Bart's. "You remember everything about that day, too, don't you?"

"I remember everything that's ever happened between us, from the time we were kids." Leaning back, Bart's expression sobered. "This house is so empty without the twins, I've been going crazy. I don't have to contend with wet towels in the bathroom, dirty dishes in the sink, music loud enough to wake the dead and a laundry room that seemed to manufacture its own supply of dirty clothes, and I hate it.''

"The chicks have left the nest," Torey commented quietly. "I wondered if that would bother you."

"Believe it or not, I never even thought about that aspect of the kids going off to school." Bart's gaze never left Torey. "Being completely alone accomplished one positive thing, though. It gave me a lot of time to think."

Torey was petting the purring cat, although she wasn't looking at Corky. She really wasn't able to look anywhere but at Bart. Emotion had filled her breast, so much so that it made her voice husky. "You're not angry with me anymore?"

"Anger wasn't what kept me away from you all summer, it was stubbornness. And maybe a little stupidity mixed in, too."

The admission was an important concession, Torey realized. "You're being very candid."

"I'd like that from you, too. Are you able to be completely honest with me?"

There was a note of anxiety in Bart's voice, as though he wasn't sure if her honesty would be in his favor. It amazed her that he was willing to risk a putdown. That inner vulnerability she'd discovered early in the summer was showing, and Bart even seemed like he wanted her to see it. Hope became dominant in the hodge-podge of Torey's thoughts.

"I can be honest with you," she stated simply.

Bart changed directions, surprising her. "I don't think you know this, Torey, but I wanted to be a doctor, too."

She didn't correct him. Perhaps Bart thought no one knew of, or maybe remembered, his youthful career aspiration.

"It started when I was in high school," Bart continued. "Do you remember Dr. Lambert?"

Torey nodded. Dr. Lambert had treated her grandmother at one time, but the elderly physician had died quite a few years ago. "I remember Dr. Lambert very well."

"He hired me to do odd jobs around his office, and he was the person who got me interested in medicine. He let me borrow his medical books and would talk to me for hours about the profession. He was already gravely ill when my dad died. I was in my third year of college when Dad had a fatal heart attack. For a few weeks everything was mass confusion. The twins were only eight year old and devastated. I tried to figure out a way to take care of them and stay in school, too, but when the state got involved and wanted to put the boys in a foster home, I knew I had to come back to the ranch for good."

Torey got a painfully acute picture of what Bart must have gone through during that sad period. "I'm so sorry," she murmured, recalling Lorna's personal remorse over waiting so long to get involved in the Scanlons' lives.

"I've never regretted it. My brothers are more important to me than any career ever could have been. But it's recently occurred to me—" Bart grinned, giving Torey a glimpse of the devil that apparently still lurked within him "—probably because this damned rain made logging impossible and I've paced this empty house so many miles it's a wonder I haven't worn out the floor. Anyway, there have been only two things I've ever really wanted, Torey." The grin completely vanished. "I willingly gave up my education. I'm not going to give up the other."

Her throat was suddenly as dry as old rope, putting a ragged edge on her voice. "Which is?"

Bart's reply was immediate. "You."

They stared at each other for what seemed like an eternity. Torey felt like she'd just been struck by lightning. She had been hoping, yes, but Bart's directness still startled her. He was waiting, she saw, watching her closely, checking her reaction.

Her mind raced. For weeks, almost two months, she had lived with a decision that was spiritually honorable but emotionally demoralizing. Could she enforce it again if Bart should ask her to do otherwise? If he should suddenly get off of the couch, close the gap between them and take her in his arms, would she stop him?

The answer was no, Torey realized. She loved him. She'd attempted to alter the course of their relationship, but the summer had been the most painful of her life. If Bart wanted her, he could have her, any way he should say, and that included a long-term affair. She simply couldn't battle herself and him, too, any longer.

With her heart in her throat, Torey broke the heavy silence. "What about your commitment to the twins?"

"That's inviolable."

"Of course. I only meant..." Biting her lip, Torey's voice trailed off. Bart had stood up and was walking around the coffee table. He stood beside Torey's chair, and she tilted her head back to look up at him.

"I can't stop wanting you," he said softly. "This summer has been a travesty and I've been a damned fool. I actually kept thinking you'd come around. I kept remembering that it was you who started this thing with us, and I thought sure it was stronger than your high-mindedness."

"It was... it is," Torey whispered, admitting again that she wasn't able to deny either of them anymore.

"Then why...?"

"Why didn't I come around? Probably for the same reason you stayed away from me, stubbornness and pride."

With only a small hesitation, Bart lifted Corky from Torey's lap and set the yellow cat on the floor. Then he took

Torey's hand and brought her to her feet. He cradled her face in his big hands and looked down at her, his expression warm and guileless. "You asked me if I loved you," he murmured huskily.

"Yes," she whispered.

"I resented that. I didn't want to be forced into anything." Bart's lips touched hers softly. "I thought I could take you or leave you," he whispered. "I can't. The choice isn't mine, which seems crazy, but it's true."

Hot emotions were swirling in Torey. It had been too long, and Bart's nearness, his hands on her, the brushing contact of their mouths, was turning her limbs to soft rubber. "I have no choices left, either," she whispered, running her hands up the hard muscles of his arms. "Whether you love me or not, Bart, I love you. I fought it all summer. I have no fight left."

She felt his body shuddering as he dropped his hands from her face and encircled her in a fierce embrace. "I love you, too. Damn, I love you. I love you so much, I can't see straight."

Tears seared Torey's eyes and began to overflow. She didn't want to be blubbering at a time like this, but the tears just kept coming.

"I think I always have, Torey. Even when we were kids. You were always just out of reach, and so damned desirable it drove me nuts. I was afraid to call you today. I was afraid you'd tell me to go to hell. I wouldn't have blamed you if you had, either."

She was being held so tightly she could hardly breathe. "It never even occurred to me to tell you to go to hell," she whispered, her voice thick with tears. She could feel how aroused he was. His body was hard and hot and reminding her of the joy of making love with him. Torey moved her cheek against his chest, drying her tears on his shirt. "I hate ultimatums, and you can't imagine how many times I wanted to run over here and tell you I was wrong."

"It couldn't have been any more often than my private battles," he said grimly, taking her shoulders and moving her back enough to see her face. "I want you to know something. That boast I made about sex not being scarce...there hasn't been any other woman, Torey, not since our first evening together."

She couldn't help the relieved breath she pulled into her lungs. "I'm very glad. I haven't dated anyone all summer, either."

Bart's voice became very quiet, very low. "Will you go upstairs with me?"

"Yes. I'd go anywhere with you. I love you."

A hot light ignited in his eyes. "You really do?"

"I really do."

Bart bent over and picked her up, swinging her up into his arms. Sighing, Torey put her arms around his neck and laid her face on his shoulder. "When I came here last spring, you asked me to go upstairs with you," she said softly.

He began the flight up with a smile touched by amusement. "As I recall, I shocked the hell out of you."

"Later, I wished I had said yes."

He cast her a heated glance. "I wished you had said yes, too. It was raining and the twins were gone, and after you left, I wandered around and tortured myself with what might have been. I knew it was hopeless, though, and that I'd never find out what having you was like."

She smiled. "But then you did find out."

They had reached Bart's bedroom, and he let Torey's feet slide to the floor. With his hands on her waist, he drew her forward. "Ah, yes, I did find out."

Torey began unbuttoning his shirt, exposing a little more hair and bronzed muscle with each button. Bart was watching her, content to let her take the lead. "Do you know how beautiful you are?" he asked, restrained hunger thickening his voice.

She looked him in the eyes. "You're very beautiful, too."

He exhibited a crooked grin. "How could I be beautiful? That's a woman's word, honey."

Parting the panels of his shirt, Torey pressed her lips to his bare chest. Her voice was low and compelling. "Take my word for it, Bart. You're the most beautiful thing I've ever seen." She licked a nipple, lingering on it, wetting it with her tongue, and Bart's hands rose to her head, his fingers twisting into her hair.

"Oh, baby," he whispered.

Her lips moved up to his throat. "I'm on fire for you," she whispered. "Burning for you."

"I know just how to put that fire out."

"I know you do. You create the fire, then you extinguish it. Only you, Bart. No other man has ever made me feel what you do."

Drawing a ragged breath, Bart reached for the hem of her sweater. "Let's get rid of some of these clothes." He lifted the garment over Torey's head and tossed it onto a chair. His expression became hot and sensual. "You're not wearing a bra." His hands opened around her breasts. "You create a fire in me, too," he rasped hoarsely.

With a harsh, guttural groan, he yanked her into his arms, flattening her breasts into his chest. "Oh, what you do to me," he growled.

She knew what she did to him. His jeans were so full of what she did to him, she marvelled that their seams held. They were breathing erratically, both of them, stealing kisses, touching, caressing. Torey's hands squeezed down in between them to Bart's belt buckle. It was only kind to release him, she felt, although the real reason for unzipping his fly was purely selfish: She wanted to see him, to touch him.

When she succeeded and was holding and stroking him, Bart, with his eyes closed, growled deep in his chest with pleasure. He enjoyed the arousing sensation of her hands for as long as he dared, then opened his eyes. "I won't last with much more of that." He reached for the button on her slacks.

Quickly now, they finished undressing. Bart threw the covers back and they lay down together. Naked, the feverish chafing of their bare skin was another tantalizing delight. Torey ran the sole of her foot up and down the length of his hair-roughened legs while their kisses became more frantic, more demanding.

"There's so much I want to do to you," Bart groaned. "But it's been too long, honey. I can't wait."

"Don't wait," she gasped. "I don't want you to wait. Make love to me, Bart."

Swiftly he moved into position, spreading her thighs wider to accommodate him. Her body was hot and wet and ready, and his entry was one long slide of utter bliss. Each emitted a rapturous cry, each took up an immediate, exhilarating rhythm. They moved as one entity, joined at their core, with each thrust a rising crescendo of unleashed desire.

Talking about their love, facing and admitting it had added a new element to their lovemaking. It was as if they were trying to brand one another with passion.

Bart's mouth left hers to harshly gulp air, and then he began to growl out his feelings. "I want to love you...love you...love you...until we both drop. Every morning, every night . . . I'll never get enough of you . . . never."

She felt the same. Her mind was bursting with love and with the wild sexuality of their coupling. They rode the crest of the wave together, and Torey went over the top first, crying out as the flames in her body gave way to spasms of pure ecstasy. They continued, weakening her voice to soft moans while Bart attained his own supreme moment.

The aftermath of total fulfillment settled upon them and it was several minutes before either could speak.

Bart raised his head, and his eyes were somnolent with satisfaction. "I love you," he breathed.

"I love you." He kept staring at her. Torey smiled and lifted her fingertips to his mouth in a tender caress. "You're staring, darling."

"I want to marry you."

Every cell in Torey's body contracted with the quick breath she took. "Is that a proposal?"

"I don't know. Maybe. I want you in my bed every night. I want you with *me,* not living on the next ranch."

Blood began pounding in Torey's head. Bart's expression didn't invite levity. He was deadly serious, obviously struggling with a situation that hadn't changed just because they were in bed together again.

Except for talking about love, of course. That was a major change, certainly a positive step toward an interwoven future.

"Would you marry me if I asked?"

Utter astonishment struck Torey. "Do you doubt it?" she returned, her eyes wide with disbelief.

"We'd have so many hurdles to get past."

"Probably no more than other couples do," Torey said carefully. "Our hurdles might be somewhat different, but I doubt that too many couples start a marriage with everything lined up and perfect."

"Do you really think that's true?"

Torey was trying to appear calm about this, but Bart was still lying on top of her. They were still as joined as they'd been in the throes of lovemaking that had been more fantastic than any she could ever have imagined in her wildest fantasies. Added to that, he was talking about marriage. The potent combination was making it tough to even breathe normally, let alone speak calmly.

"Do you want to talk about it, Bart?"

His eyes narrowed slightly, and after a pause, he startled Torey by exclaiming, "No, I don't want to talk about it. What I want to do is propose. I should have done it two months ago. Will you marry me, Torey?"

"Of course I'll marry you," she said, then threw her arms around his neck. "I decided today that I would carry on an affair with you until we were both old and gray, if that's what you wanted. But marriage! Yes, yes, yes."

He laughed joyously and hugged her. "I love you. We'll work things out, Torey, whatever it takes. It won't be easy sometimes. I've got years of hard work and long hours ahead of me, but I think we'll make it. Lord, I've been an idiot. What if you had gone back to Steve what's-his-name?"

Torey laughed, too. "I suppose you've forgotten his last name again?"

"You're on to me now, aren't you?" Bart chuckled. "We're going to be a happy family, Torey. You, me, Lorna and the twins."

"And those three killers guarding your house and Corky," she reminded happily, profoundly pleased that Bart had included Lorna in that lovely picture. After a second she added softly, "And maybe some babies?" She felt a tremor ripple through his body, and a dart of fear pierced her heart at the thought that maybe Bart didn't count on babies as part of their future. "Do you want children?"

Bart cleared his throat. "At least seven."

"Seven!" Torey tilted her head back to give him a wide-eyed look. "Seven children are..." She saw the deviltry in his eyes. "You're teasing me, aren't you?"

Laughing, Bart dropped a kiss on the end of her nose. "Honey, next to making love to you, there isn't anything I enjoy more than teasing you. Do you really want me to stop?"

Torey pressed her lips to his throat. "What I really want is for you to make love to me again," she whispered, then looked up at him with an innocent face. "Or, is it too soon?"

Bart's expression changed from lighthearted to sober, and he moved seductively. "What do you think? We can while away this whole rainy afternoon...."

She sighed. "Yes, oh yes, my love."

*　　*　　*　　*　　*

BEGINNING IN FEBRUARY FROM

SILHOUETTE Desire™

Western Lovers

An exciting new series by Elizabeth Lowell
Three fabulous love stories
Three sexy, tough, tantalizing heroes

In February,   *Man of the Month* Tennessee Blackthorne in
              OUTLAW
In March,   Cash McQueen in *GRANITE MAN*
In April,   Nevada Blackthorne in *WARRIOR*

WESTERN LOVERS—Men as tough and untamed as
the land they call home.

Only in *Silhouette Desire!*

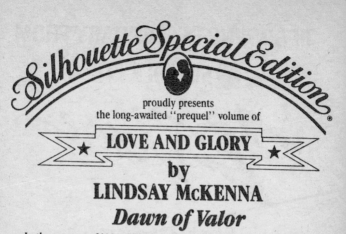

Silhouette Special Edition

proudly presents
the long-awaited "prequel" volume of

★ LOVE AND GLORY ★

by
LINDSAY McKENNA
Dawn of Valor

In the summer of '89, Silhouette Special Edition premiered three novels celebrating America's men and women in uniform: LOVE AND GLORY, by bestselling author Lindsay McKenna. Featured were the proud Trayherns, a military family as bold and patriotic as the American flag—three siblings valiantly battling the threat of dishonor, determined to triumph . . . in love and glory.

Now, discover the roots of the Trayhern brand of courage, as parents Chase and Rachel relive their earliest heartstopping experiences of survival and indomitable love, in

Dawn of Valor, Silhouette Special Edition #649

This month, experience the thrill of LOVE AND GLORY—from the very beginning!

Silhouette Books®

DV-1A

Take 4 bestselling love stories FREE

Plus get a FREE surprise gift!

SILHOUETTE·INTIMATE·MOMENTS®

NORA ROBERTS
Night Shadow

People all over the city of Urbana were asking, Who was that masked man?

Assistant district attorney Deborah O'Roarke was the first to learn his secret identity . . . and her life would never be the same.

The stories of the lives and loves of the O'Roarke sisters began in January 1991 with NIGHT SHIFT, Silhouette Intimate Moments #365. And if you want to know more about Deborah and the man behind the mask, look for NIGHT SHADOW, Silhouette Intimate Moments #373, available in March at your favorite retail outlet.

NITE-1